DARKNESS
BEFORE
DAWN

SHARON M. DRAPER

DARKNESS
BEFORE
DAWN

Simon Pulse

New York London Toronto Sydney Singapore

First Simon Pulse edition July 2002

SIMON PULSE
An Imprint of Simon & Schuster
Children's Publishing Division
1230 Avenue of the Americas
New York, NY 10020

Also available in an Atheneum Books for Young Readers hardcover edition.
Designed by Sammy Yuen Jr.
The text of this book was set in Cheltenham

Printed in the United States of America
10 9 8 7 6 5 4

The Library of Congress has cataloged the hardcover edition as follows:
HC data
Draper, Sharon M.   Darkness before dawn/by Sharon M. Draper   p.   cm.
Summary: Recovering from the recent suicide of her ex-boyfriend, senior class president Keisha Montgomery finds herself attracted to a dangerous, older man.
ISBN 0-689-83080-7 (hc)
[1. High schools—Fiction. 2. Schools—Fiction. 3. Rape—Fiction.
R. Afro-Americans—Fiction.] I. Title
PZ7.D78325 Be2001   [Fic]—dc21   99-058860

ISBN: 0-689-85134-0 (pbk.)

To all the young readers who wrote me letters and asked me questions about what happened to the characters from *Tears of a Tiger* and *Forged by Fire*. Because of you, the characters were allowed to live and grow and develop into real personalities. Because of you, they will never die.

Thank you.

—Sharon M. Draper

We wait in the darkness for the signal to begin. I wonder what's taking so long. Behind me, I hear somebody whispering. Our silky gowns are rustling softly as we, the graduating seniors, adjust our hats, hair, and nerves. We stand nervously in two lines that curve from the back of the auditorium, out into the hallway, and halfway up a flight of stairs. In alphabetical order for the very last time, the boys in gowns of navy blue, the girls in silver.

I'm one of the first in line because I have to sit on the stage. Even though it's hot, I'm shivering in the darkness while we wait for the lights to come up to announce the beginning of the ceremony. I close my eyes, but the darkness seems like it's trying to grab me. I blink, and the shadows are breathing on my neck, chasing through my thoughts.

I let the shadows walk me back through the last two years, through loss, pain, death, and humiliation. I've got dark memories of fire and blood running in slow motion through my head. I think about Rob, who died in a car crash in November of our junior year. I think about my Andy, my dear sweet Andy, who left me—left us all—the following April. And I try not to think about my own dark stain that I know will never be erased.

Like silent trumpets, the lights of the auditorium suddenly blaze. We seniors cheer, the audience stands and applauds, and then we hear the tinny sound of "Pomp and Circumstance" coming from the school orchestra sitting down front. I always cry when I hear that song. As we march proudly down the aisle in the procession, excited parents flashing cameras and waving with joy, I think back to my first day of school as a kindergartner, how scared I was, and how a skinny little boy named Andy Jackson shared his peanut butter sandwich with me. I think about grade school and long division, junior high and locker partners, high school and basketball games, hospitals and funerals.

As senior class president, I have to give a speech tonight, but I don't know if I'm going to be able to stand in front of this huge room of parents and students and put the shadows into words. I climb the steps slowly—this is no time to trip or stumble—and I watch the others march in. The rest of the graduates proudly file into rows of gowns and hats into the seats in front of me, their faces unwrapped packages of smiles and success. We sit down and the ceremony begins with the usual speeches from school board members and declarations by the principal. My speech is the very last of the evening—our final good-bye. I hold the pages tightly in my hand as I skim the words once more. I try to relax a little, and I grab the tiny butterfly that hangs from the thin silver chain around my neck. I take a deep breath and I finally let myself think about everything that's happened. I let the shadows take me back to last year—to that day in April—the day that Andy died.

1

I think homeroom is a stupid waste of time. They take attendance, read announcements, then make you sit in a room watching the clock when you could be in a class, maybe even learning something. Dumb! Mr. Whitfield is okay as a teacher—he's probably too nice, so kids take advantage of him sometimes, like I'm getting ready to do.

"Grimes?"

"Here."

"Hawkins?"

"Yeah."

"Henderson?"

"Here."

"Immerman?"

"Over here."

"Jackson? . . . Jackson? . . . Is Andy absent again?"

Everybody looked at me like I'm supposed to know where Andy is at every single moment. I'm not his mother. I'm not even his girlfriend anymore. I ignored them all and dug in my book bag for a pencil.

"Yeah, Mr. Whitfield. He's got 'senioritis,' a terrible disease." Leon thinks he's so funny. Everybody laughed but me.

"Well, since he's only a junior, I'd say that he's got a fatal disease. Juniors who catch senioritis have been known to develop serious complications and never graduate," Mr. Whitfield said jokingly.

"He'll be here tomorrow. He has to. He owes me two dollars."

"Good luck. Okay, let's finish with attendance."

"Johnson, Ranita?"

"Here . . ."

"Montgomery, Keisha?"

"I'm here. Mr. Whitfield? I don't feel good. Can I go to the nurse?"

"Okay, Keisha, but unless you're going home, try to get back in a hurry."

I wasn't really sick. I shouldered my book bag and headed out of the room without looking at Mr. Whitfield. I was still upset about breaking up with Andy, and I just needed some space. I glanced down to the end of the hall where I saw my best friend Rhonda heading my way. She yelled down the hall, "Hey, Keisha, have you seen Andy this morning?" A couple of teachers stuck their heads out of their doors, but Rhonda ignored them as she hurried down the hall toward me.

"No, and I hope I never do again."

"Come on, girl, you don't really mean that. I know it hurts. You and Andy were together for so long. It's hard on me to see you two break up."

"Yeah, Rhonda. It hurts. I really liked him, you know, but it just got too complicated. He's better off without me. He's got to get himself together before he can get seriously involved with someone else. How's Tyrone?"

"Oh, just fine—so fine!" Rhonda giggled. "We're going to the movies tomorrow. Do you want to come?"

"No, I'll probably just catch a movie on cable. It's kinda nice just to relax for a change and not worry about how I look or what I'll wear or where we're going. I'm just going to chill and enjoy my freedom." I said the words, but Rhonda knew I didn't mean them.

"Okay, but call me if you change your mind. Say, I'm going to drop off Andy's chemistry homework at his house after school. Mr. Whitfield said he'd fail unless he got this assignment in. You wouldn't want to go with me, would you?"

"No way, girl. Actually, if I saw him, I might break down and do something stupid like cry, or make up with him. I'm out of his life—at least for now."

"Okay. I'll call you later."

When Rhonda had called me later that night, however, she was crying hysterically about Andy and blood and a gun. She wasn't making any sense at all.

"Oh, Keisha! It's Andy!"

"What about him?"

"Blood everywhere!"

"Where? What are you talking about?"

"Monty. Poor little Monty. He found him."

"Found who?"

"He found Andy."

"Is Andy okay?"

"He had a gun! His father's hunting rifle!"

"Who did?"

"Andy!"

"Calm down and tell me what's goin' on! You're not making any sense!"

"Andy's dead, Keisha. He shot himself. Monty found him when he got home from school. I got there about the same time Andy's mom got home. It was awful! Oh, Keisha!" Rhonda dropped the phone and all I could hear was heavy, choked sobs coming from her. I didn't cry right then. But it felt like a huge rock landed inside my chest and just sat there. I didn't want to believe her, but

8

soon it was clear that it was all too true. Andy had taken his own life.

I felt dead, too. Like living was stealing breath. I felt like it was my fault, even though I knew it wasn't. Andy had been really messed up inside since that terrible car crash last year after a basketball game. Andy had been driving the car and had been drinking. His best friend Rob Washington had died. I guess he just couldn't get over his feeling of guilt for Robbie's death. I also knew that part of the mess in Andy's head had to do with us breaking up, but I wasn't gonna be caught up in that same guilt trip. I felt like I was going to explode.

I heard the door open downstairs; my mom had just come in from work. I ran to her and screamed, "Mom, oh Mommy, Andy's dead!" I let her hug me like she used to do when I was little. My nose was all stopped up and all I could do was gulp and sniff and cry some more. "It's all my fault!" I moaned. "How could he do this? Why didn't he call me? Andy can't be dead! Oh, Mommy, it hurts so bad!" I couldn't stop crying. I never knew a person had so many tears inside.

As she heard the news, my mom gasped and held me real close. I think she cried, too. She let me sob like a baby; I could feel her strength and love. She stroked my hair and soothed me with the same whispers and mother tones that had calmed me since I was a little girl. When my sobbing had slowed down a little, she gave me a couple of tissues and said quietly, "Tell me what happened, Keisha."

"I'm not sure. They just found him." I sat on the sofa next to my mother with my head in my hands. I just couldn't stop crying. "Why didn't he call me? Even though we broke up, he knew I still loved him. He knew I'd talk him through any problem."

"He did call," my mother said quietly. She was really crying now.

I looked up at her in disbelief. "When?" I asked suddenly.

"Last night, well after midnight. You were asleep, and I didn't want to wake you, and I thought it could wait until morning. I'm so sorry, Keisha."

"Mom!" I shouted. "How could you be so cold?" I jumped up and glared at her. My eyes, which were already red and burning from all the crying, felt like hot swords as I glared at her.

"I couldn't possibly have known, Keisha," Mom said gently. "I couldn't possibly have known," she repeated, weeping quietly into her hands. "I'm so sorry."

I looked at my mother with a mixture of disgust and rage. I had to get out of there. "I have to get to Andy's house," I said suddenly.

"I have to see for myself. And I have to see Monty. He's going to need somebody. Can I use your car, Mom? I'll be careful."

"Let me drive you, Keisha. You're too upset and shaken to drive. Besides, Andy's parents are going to need some support, too."

"I guess you're right. Let's hurry." My voice was tight and I avoided the offer of a final hug from my mother. I pretended not to notice my mother's outstretched arms as I looked for the car keys, and I refused to look her in the eye as we walked out the door. I was silent as we rode to Andy's house.

When we got there, at least six police cars crowded Andy's little street and a bright red ambulance sat in the driveway, red lights blinking in the dusk. Crowds of kids from school huddled together. Even boys were crying without embarrassment on the front lawn, and girls sobbed together, using each other for support. Rhonda sat on the damp lawn with Tyrone, pulling blades of grass from the earth, one at a time, unable to cry anymore, I guess. Her eyes were red and swollen like mine. Tyrone sat very close to her, his arm resting on her leg, looking like he was barely holding in his own tears and anger. He and Andy had played together on the Hazelwood High School basketball team, and had been friends since seventh grade.

I sat down next to Rhonda and hugged

her. "I feel so helpless!" I sobbed. "Why did he do this to me?"

"He didn't do it to you, Keisha," Tyrone said quietly. "He did it to himself."

"No, Tyrone," I flashed back at him. "He did it to all of us!" I couldn't look at Tyrone anymore. I hated that Rhonda had Tyrone there to hold and comfort her, while I had no one.

Gerald, another friend and basketball teammate, arrived with his fourteen-year-old sister, Angel. His face was twisted with confusion; Angel was sobbing and sniffling. I walked over to Angel, hugged her, and let her cry. Poor kid. Angel and Gerald had already been through more than their share of unhappiness and death. I glanced over at Gerald, whose face thanked me silently for trying to comfort his sister.

"I ain't got over Robbie bein' dead," Gerald told me quietly. "High school boys ain't supposed to die. They're supposed to act stupid, and flunk tests, and chase girls, and get out of school, and live. Not die. And now Andy is dead, too? I can't deal with this!" He clenched his fists.

I couldn't say anything. He was right.

Just then another car pulled up and Rob's fourteen-year-old sister, Kiara, rushed out of the car and over to Angel. I watched as the two friends ran to each other and wept as they tried to console each other. So many tears.

I said to Gerald, "You know this is hard on Kiara. She hasn't gotten over her own big brother's death."

"Yeah, I feel you. Nothing but Band-Aids covering all that pain, and this must rip everything raw for her."

I sighed and said carefully, "This must be rough on both of you. You two have been through more mess than oughta be allowed."

"Yeah." Gerald glanced at the sky, which was almost completely dark now. "Leftover pain to the max."

I touched him gently on the shoulder. "I feel ya. It's going to be rough for Monty and his folks, too. Poor kid. He just turned seven."

I could see Andy and Monty's parents through the front window, huddled together on the sofa. My mom went in and sat with them, once again offering her shoulder as a pillow for pain. Policemen marched in and out of the house, barking orders into their shoulder radios.

I didn't notice Monty at first. He was sitting alone in a swing on the lawn of the house across the street. I left Gerald, wiped my eyes and breathed deeply, and walked slowly across the street to Monty. When me and Andy used to study together at his house, Monty's bright eyes and crooked-toothed grin always greeted me at the door. But what do you say to a second grader who's just found his brother's body?

"Hey, Monty," I said quietly. He didn't answer. He was wearing Andy's school jacket, the one that said Hazelwood High in large, shiny silver letters. "You need a hug?" I asked.

Monty nodded slightly. I sat down next to him and held him gently in my arms. I pushed with my feet and let the swing rock us both gently. Neither of us spoke. I felt Monty relax a little and I hugged him closer to me. The evening air was cool; the early spring sun had left little warmth. As the day ended and the night took control, me and Monty cried together in the swing. We kinda shielded each other from the wails of the kids as the plastic bag that contained what had once been Andy was removed from the house. The ambulance left with blinking lights, but no siren, and everyone was left with only darkness and silence.

It was then that Monty's mother frantically called out to him from the house. I guess she realized she hadn't seen him in a while and got worried. Reluctantly, he gave me one last hug, left the swing, and ran across the street to his mother, the arms of Andy's jacket dragging the ground.

2

The rest of that school year was almost impossible for everybody. The school brought in grief counselors, just as they had when Robbie had died five months before. They were strangers, though, asking questions that no one could answer. They tried to be helpful, but we were glad when they left. We had our own way of dealing with grief. We went to Eden Park together and sat by the reflecting pool and talked about stuff that was bothering us. Rhonda and Tyrone got so tight that I think they were braided together. He'd breathe out and she'd breathe in. I didn't have anybody, and that's the way I wanted it. I didn't think I would ever find anyone else. I'd known Andy since kindergarten. How could someone come and replace eleven years of memories?

It was time for the all-school picnic. I remember sighing as I packed a bag to take— a deck of cards, a can of bug spray, a Frisbee, even my swimming suit, but I doubted if I would swim this year. This picnic was always the best part of the school year. On the Saturday after the last day of school, everybody went to Houston Woods State Park, where we had races and games, cooked hot dogs and hamburgers on the grill, rented paddleboats and rowboats, sang songs and told ghost stories by the fire until midnight. Teachers brought their own kids, students brought their little brothers and sisters, and all the hard work of the school year was forgotten in the flickering of the bonfire at the end of the day. Andy and I had always taken Monty along. He wouldn't sleep for a week in anticipation.

I decided to call Monty to see if he'd like to go with me this year.

"I'm scared to go, Keisha," Monty admitted after a silence.

"Why, Monty?"

"'Cause Andy won't be there," Monty said quietly. "And I'm scared of the ghost stories."

"We can leave before dark. I promise."

"But the fire in the dark is the best part." Monty was worried. "Keisha?" he asked.

"Yes, Monty."

"Is Andy a ghost now?"

I saw now what was frightening Monty. "No, Monty, I don't think so," I said honestly. "Andy is in a good place, where he is happy and at peace. Besides, ghosts aren't real and Andy is real. He will always be real as long as you love him and I love him."

"Are you sure?" Monty asked.

"As sure as I can be, Monty. I know that Andy misses you as much as you miss him. But come to the picnic with me. There'll be lots of other kids there, and you need to have some fun. Tell your mom I'll pick you up at three."

"Okay, Keisha. Thanks."

When we got to the picnic, most of my friends were already there. B. J. was sitting under a tree with the smallest children, telling them stories and helping them sing songs. I waved at him, and he waved back, smiling. B. J. was either going to be a preacher or a teacher—everybody said so. He loved kids, especially the younger ones. Maybe that's because they were smaller than he was. B. J. was only five feet tall, but he was tough and wiry and knew tae kwon do. Kids seemed to collect around him wherever he went. He had managed to collect several younger siblings of the senior class, as well as several children of faculty members. The five-year-old twins of

Mr. Jasper, the art teacher, each grabbed one of B. J.'s hands as they dragged him to where their dad was painting the faces of the little ones. He grinned at me as the kids pushed him into Mr. Jasper's lawn chair and he pretended to protest as tiger stripes were painted on his cheeks.

The principal, Mr. Hathaway, was cheerfully grilling hamburgers. With him was a young man who was obviously his son, but I'd never seen him before. Mr. Hathaway was tall, with caramel-colored skin. He had probably been good-looking thirty years before, and had very unusual hazel, almost golden eyes. Andy used to tease the freshmen and tell them that Hathaway had X-ray vision, because nothing seemed to get by him; those eyes seemed to pierce right into a kid who got caught doing something wrong. Mr. Hathaway's son, who was delivering ice and soda to his father, looked like a younger, tighter version of his dad. He was muscular, slim, and strikingly good looking, for his hazel eyes decorated perfectly his honey-bronzed face. His movements, as he lifted the heavy boxes, reminded me of water flowing down a mountain—powerful and strong, but gentle— almost liquid. I glanced at him, not really interested, but he sure did look good. He flashed a smile at me which I guess was meant to charm me. Didn't work. My mama taught me to be polite, so I smiled back. Now, I'm no fool—he was really fine—but he looked to be way over twenty-one, so he disappeared from my thoughts about as fast as his smile faded. I didn't look back, but I was aware he was watching me as I headed over with Monty to speak to Mrs. Blackwell, my English teacher, who had brought her son Brandon.

Brandon was eight, and he challenged Monty to a foot race right away. I laughed as I watched them run across the grass. Monty left Brandon in the dust and roared with delight as he took his victory lap around a tree. Brandon laughed and tried to trip him. Then both boys wandered down to watch the junior high girls play softball. I walked alone, remembering the places Andy and I had walked last year. The sun was warm, and I felt relaxed and at peace for the moment. I walked over to watch the game.

Angel sat on the bench with Rob's younger sister, Kiara, who now insisted on being called Joyelle. Neither of them showed much excitement about the girls' softball game. Kiara had called me a few days after Andy's funeral.

"Can I ask you something serious, Keisha?" she had asked. I could hear the tremor in her voice.

"Sure," I replied. "Are you okay?"

"No, not really. I'll probably never be okay

again," she said. "I miss my brother, I'm still shaking about Andy, and I'm scared death is just gonna jump in and grab me, too!"

"I know it's hard," I told her, "but you gotta hold on to the good memories and step out into the future—even if it's scary. That's what I'm trying to do."

"I'm trying to grab hold of something," Kiara replied. "And I decided I'm changing my name," she said suddenly, breathing deeply into the phone. "What do you think?"

"Huh? Can you do that?"

"I have to do something, or I'll go crazy," Kiara explained. "My parents can't get past Robbie's death and I can't either. And now with Andy being gone, too, I think I'm gonna explode! I have to change something so I can deal with tomorrow, like you said. Do you feel me on this?"

"Yeah, I feel you, I guess. What are you gonna change it to?"

"I've been thinking about this a lot," Kiara replied. "Robbie and Andy used to call me by my full name to tease me, but I kinda liked it. It made me feel like an actress or a movie star or somebody who gives autographs to other people."

"What is your full name?"

"Kiara Joyelle Leila Victoria Washington."

"That's a mouthful," I commented.

"I just want to be called Joyelle. Is that

too much to ask?" She started to cry again. "I want some joy in my life—all the time," she said angrily. "If anybody wants to talk to me, they have to call me with joy on their lips when they do," she added almost defiantly.

"I think that's cool, Joyelle," I told her. All she wanted was for someone to tell her it was okay. "I got your back on this."

"Thanks, Keisha. This is important to me. I'm gonna tell my parents as soon as they get home from work."

"What will they say?"

"It will take them some time to get used to it, but they'll do it. It's cheaper than taking me to a shrink, which is probably what *they* need. Life is rough at my house."

As Joyelle had predicted, her parents let her do it. They called her what she wanted, because I think it was easier than dealing with the kid's pain. I glanced at the two friends watching the game. They looked so bored they could have been in math class. Angel was thin, pale, and almost ghostlike, while Joyelle was round, brown, and solid. Angel was tall; Joyelle was short. But they fit together like coffee and cream. Both of them had started paying more attention to the high school boys playing on the next field than to their own game. They giggled as they watched Gerald miss a hit and Tyrone miss a catch. I just smiled as I watched the boys try to cover their mistakes with loud, macho grunts and roars.

"I can play better than that," Monty boasted as he walked to the fence.

"Go for it, Monty!" I challenged. "I bet you can, too!"

"Why don't you go on out there and show them!" Angel told him with a laugh.

Joyelle laughed, too, as Monty sauntered over to the field. He picked up a bat and stepped in front of the next batter. "Play ball!" he yelled.

The boys on the field, mostly juniors and seniors, cracked up as the seven year old spit in the dirt. "Throw him your fast ball, Gerald!" Leon yelled from the outfield. Leon could always get a laugh from kids as well as teachers. When the biology teacher brought in small minnows to feed the bass in the classroom tank, Leon grabbed a minnow and swallowed it whole. The girls squealed, the boys hooted, and the teacher chuckled and told Leon to stop now or eat all three dozen minnows. Leon laughed and said he'd had enough, but he pretended to breathe like a fish with gills for the rest of the class. He, too, had been with most of them since kindergarten, but somehow he had never been part of their close group of friends.

Gerald wound up his pitch, and threw it with full force at the little boy who stood in front of him—knees bent, bat ready, determination in his eye. Monty watched the ball approach, waited for the right moment, then swung with so much power he almost twisted completely around. The ball connected with a resounding wallop and Monty took off around the bases on his short, sturdy legs. He rounded first base with ease. The older boys, who at first had been laughing, were now cheering him on as the outfield fumbled to get the ball. Monty approached second base just as the ball was thrown, but Tyrone, the second baseman, missed because he was laughing so hard, so Monty continued, full speed, to third. He passed third base seconds before the ball did, and he slid into home like the professionals he watched on TV.

Both teams exploded in cheers for him, as well as the girls from the junior high softball teams. Even though the game wasn't over, they put Monty up on their shoulders and marched him all the way back to the food area, where they all got hamburgers and soda.

Leon grabbed a burger from Mr. Hathaway's grill and fixed it with onions, potato chips, and baked beans stuffed under the bun, which Monty gobbled with glee. Leon then took a watermelon and cracked it open by bringing it down with full force on the corner of the picnic table with a loud sploosh. "I've always wanted to do that!" he said with satisfaction.

"Tastes better when it's ragged!" Monty agreed, grabbing a handful of watermelon with his bare, dirty hands. Leon joined him and the two of them gobbled the sweet, red, juicy hunks of watermelon, gleefully ignoring the disgusted looks they got from some of the girls.

I got a small plate of potato salad and corn chips and sat across from them. I just shook my head at Leon and Monty.

"Want some, Keisha?" Monty asked with a grin.

"Not a chance!" I told him.

"You don't know what a good thing you're missing!" Leon said, smiling shyly. He hardly ever spoke to me at school.

I looked directly at him, which made him glance away and pretend to swat insects from the watermelon. "Something about dirty hands and watermelon juice just doesn't turn me on," I said, smiling back. Leon just laughed and dug out another huge handful of watermelon and gave it to Monty.

I nibbled at my potato salad and looked at Leon closely. He was one of those kids that you know but you never really pay much attention to. Leon was just a little taller than me, brown-skinned and rugged looking. He wasn't what the girls would call fine, but he would be at the top of our list for a second look. His eyes, which were large and dark, were accented by his heavy eyebrows. He wore his hair cut very close, and everybody knew that he could really sing. When Leon noticed me looking at him, he jumped up to get Monty some cake. He brought Monty two slices, then slapped him on the back. "You're really good, kid! Keep it up and you'll be almost as good as I am! Andy would have been very proud of you, kid." Leon wandered off then to watch the teachers play Scrabble.

Monty grinned with delight. Then his smile faded a little. I know he was thinking about Andy. He gulped and swallowed hard. I could tell he was trying not to cry.

Joyelle noticed. She walked over to him and sat down. "I know what you're thinking, Monty. It's okay to think about him. I think about Robbie all the time. Sometimes I even talk to him. And it's okay to cry. But don't cry today. You were dynamite out there!" She touched him gently on the hand. "Wasn't he, Keisha?" she asked.

"Best I've seen today!" I said honestly.

Monty sniffed and grinned at me and Joyelle. The sun was setting on the lake and the three of us sat together in silence, watching it go down, each remembering what we had lost.

Just then, Rhonda and Tyrone came laughing and chasing each other from the woods. She was dodging him like she didn't want him to catch her, and he was missing like he really couldn't. "Whassa matter, girl?" he yelled to her, laughing. "You scared to get that fine outfit all wet?"

"You are *not* gonna throw me in that water!" Rhonda squealed, dodging his outstretched arms.

"Yeah, I better not," he said as they got to the table where I was sitting. "I don't wanna have to face your mama and tell her how your new outfit got all wrinkled and shrunk! That's what happens to cheap clothes when they get wet, you know."

He ducked as she squealed and pretended to hit him, then grinned at her as he headed over to the grill to get some food.

Rhonda said down next to me, still laughing, her face glowing with perspiration and happiness. "I don't know what I'm gonna do with him," she said breathlessly.

"Love him," I replied simply.

Rhonda glanced at me and said quietly, "That's part of the problem. I gotta talk to you, girl." We walked over to a bench by the lake, leaving Monty and Joyelle arguing over the last piece of cake.

"What's up?" I asked. Me and Rhonda have been tight since seventh grade when we were assigned as locker partners. Even though I'm sorta serious and studious, and Rhonda uses the "no stress/no strain" attitude toward school, we've stayed close all through high school.

Rhonda sighed. "It's Tyrone."

"He's not creepin' around, is he?" I asked.

"No way. It's just the opposite. I like him so much, and he feels the same way and sometimes I feel like I'm gonna explode 'cause I want him so bad. And he wants me, too. I don't know what to do."

I sighed. Andy and I had once felt that way—it seemed so long ago. "Did anything happen just now?" I knew this wasn't just lazy girl talk. Rhonda and Tyrone had been gone from the group for quite a while.

Rhonda sighed and nodded. "We were sitting right over there on that log, watching the sun as it slowly went down. Looked like a big red piece of candy. I'm feeling real mellow, then he reaches over and kisses me—real sweet and tender-like. Then he kissed me again. And another time. It's like the kisses came so fast that one just melted into the other."

"And you felt like you were melting into him as well," I added, remembering.

"Oh, yeah." Rhonda closed her eyes and remembered. "He was fire. I was wax."

"And you both felt like a puddle of hot sauce," I said with a smile. I knew. I had been there.

"'I love you, Rhonda,' he told me then," Rhonda continued. "So I told him, 'I love you, too, Tyrone.' I touched his face and traced the scar on his cheek. It's almost gone—you know, the one he got from the accident."

"I know which one," I replied real quietly.

"This isn't upsetting you, is it, Keisha?" Rhonda asked with real concern. "Maybe we better get back to the picnic."

"No, girl. I'm fine. Let's just see if we can get you through this. Keep talkin'."

"You know, even though Tyrone's only got that small scar on his face, I know the scars inside are deep and ugly." Rhonda sighed and watched the shadows where the sun had disappeared. "Andy's death brought everything back to him—the night of the accident when he and Andy and B.J. watched Rob die in that car."

I started to cry.

"I wonder if Andy realized how much his death would affect so many people," Rhonda mused, reaching over to grab my hand.

"Probably not," I said, sniffing. "Andy was fighting his own monsters—he didn't have time to think about anybody else."

Rhonda added, "You know, I'm probably the only person who's seen Tyrone cry. He looks tough—like a boxer or a soldier. But he's gentle as a kitten. And he's afraid of death. I've seen him tremble."

"Seems like you do a pretty good job of making him tremble, too!" I teased her, trying to lighten the mood.

Someone's crying, Lord, kumbaya,
Oh, Lord, kumbaya.

All of them had shed many tears in the past few months. The fire and the music danced together in the darkness. Rhonda and Tyrone began the next verse together. They hadn't planned it—seems like their thoughts were really together that night.

Someone's happy, Lord, kumbaya,
Someone's happy, Lord, kumbaya,
Someone's happy, Lord, kumbaya,
Oh, Lord, kumbaya.

They looked at each other and smiled. I could tell they felt almost guilty because of their happiness. But Tyrone had told me earlier that he figured joy had to be grabbed when it was given. He had seen too much taken away in too short a time.

Gerald glanced at Angel and began the next verse. He'd give anything to make sure Angel had nothing but happiness for the rest of her life. And dancing made her happy. I had seen her perform once. She was a feather on the stage, dancing with the air and her dreams.

Someone's dancing, Lord, kumbaya,
Someone's dancing, Lord, kumbaya,
Someone's dancing, Lord, kumbaya,

Oh, Lord, kumbaya.

Leon's smooth bass drifted out of the shadows next. His voice was laced with a pain we all felt, but couldn't explain. He's so silly at school, we might have expected him to sing, "Someone's laughing, Lord," but Leon's voice came from a place we could all feel. We joined him as he sang.

Someone's hurting, Lord, kumbaya,
Someone's hurting, Lord, kumbaya,
Someone's hurting, Lord, kumbaya,
Oh, Lord, kumbaya.

After several more verses, B. J. ended it with the final verse—I know it was his favorite.

Someone's praying, Lord, kumbaya,
Someone's praying, Lord, kumbaya,
Someone's praying, Lord, kumbaya,
Oh, Lord, kumbaya.

The picnic ended not long after that. No one was much inclined to tell any ghost stories, for which I know Monty was very grateful. School was over, and summer vacation stretched ahead, long and inviting for all of us there who needed time for peace and healing.

3

"Will all seniors please rise and be recognized!" It was hot and stuffy in the auditorium on that first day of school in September, but not one of us in the senior class seemed to care. We jumped to our feet and cheered loudly—chanting *"Seniors! Seniors! Seniors!"* while we stomped and made general fools of ourselves in the front of the auditorium. It's a tradition at Hazelwood High that on the first day, the entire school meets for an assembly to welcome everyone back, review the school rules and changes for the year, and introduce the new class of seniors. Me, Rhonda, Gerald, Tyrone, and B. J. sat together in the very front row and, holding hands, stood up with the rest of our class, feeling proud and victorious that we had made it to that moment.

Leon Hawkins sat behind us. He said to me as I walked in the building that morning, "Lookin' good in that yellow! Makes you look like butter!" I guess it was a compliment, but getting compared to butter is weird. He stood up on his seat, and screamed at the top of his voice, "Hallelujah! I'm so glad I'm not a *junior* anymore!" Everybody laughed as he almost fell, and I turned around and smiled at him. He got yelled at by Mr. Jasper, the senior advisor, but Leon was used to it and ignored him.

Angel and Joyelle were new ninth graders at Hazelwood that year. They sat in the back with the freshmen. I know they were looking enviously at all of us victorious seniors in the front. I had heard them talking in the main hall that morning, looking scared and over-whelmed. Angel had whispered to Joyelle, "Do you know how much homework and note-books and reports and projects we have to do to get to be seniors?"

Joyelle nodded. "Yeah, but they were like us once. We'll get there, too."

"But that was a *long* time ago!" Angel had sighed. "We're only fourteen! I feel like such a baby!"

"I'll be fifteen next month, and your birthday is right after Christmas, so just don't tell anybody how young we are. This is high school! Fake it, sister!" Joyelle had laughed with delight.

Mr. Hathaway asked the entire room for silence, and finally quieted the jubilant seniors the way he did every year. "Remember, seniors, none of you has graduated yet. You still have nine months of education to complete and nothing is guaranteed. I expect the best from each of you or I guarantee you can expect the worst from me!"

As seniors, we'd heard his first-day speech many times before, but this time it was different, so we paid attention. Many of the announcements had to do with dates for the SAT tests, college applications, and counselor visits, along with the usual information about bus schedules, hall passes, and lunch bells. Mr. Hathaway also introduced the teachers who were new to the school. When Mr. Hathaway called them to the stage, the restless teenagers summed up each one in a glance. I could hear the whispers.

"That one is going to be mean—look at those evil eyes."

"I'll be skipping out on that one's class by the second week—she's an airhead."

"Would you look at that outfit she's wearing! What would possess her to wear purple pants and a green striped shirt?"

"We can scare her away, but we won't—she's too cute."

"How can somebody so tall be so clumsy? He tripped twice on the stage steps!"

"She looks like a kid! That's a teacher? Are they allowed to wear jeans and gym shoes like us?"

The last new person to be introduced was Mr. Hathaway's son. I glanced up in mild interest as Mr. Hathaway called him to the stage.

"He sure *looks* good! Umph! What a face! What a body!" Rhonda remarked.

"What you lookin' at, girl?" Tyrone teased. "What more can you want? You got me—the magnificent one!"

"I don't want him, Tyrone. I just recognize quality stuff when I see it. And he definitely has got the stuff!" She grinned at Tyrone and punched his arm. "And who named you the mighty magnificent one anyway?"

"I did!" He smiled.

Mr. Hathaway was smiling, too, as the young man bounded onto the stage. The auditorium echoed with the whispers of approval from the girls. He signaled for silence. "This is the final introduction of the morning."

"Glad you saved the best for last!" a girl from the back of the room yelled out.

Mr. Hathaway must have been in a good mood, because he ignored her, although the students laughed at her outburst. "This is Jonathan Hathaway, my son. He's a junior at the university, majoring in education. He'll be doing his student observation this year, and he has volunteered to help coach some of our basketball and track teams, so you'll be seeing quite a bit of him. I expect you to show him the same respect that you show me."

"Oh, he'll get more than that!" another girl yelled out. Everyone laughed, including Jonathan, who looked relaxed and comfortable. His clothes, unlike the jeans and big shirts worn by most of the boys at the school, were soft and tailored, and hung on his muscular body with ease. The first two buttons of his beige silk shirt were unfastened, and soft curly hairs from his bronzed chest peeked from the collar. His matching slacks were neatly pressed, and he brushed a minute speck of dust from them as he smiled at the crowd with confidence. Mr. Hathaway gave Jonathan a wide, proud grin but, strangely, Jonathan didn't return his father's smile.

Just before the bell was to ring to begin classes for the day, Mr. Hathaway cleared his throat and asked for silence. "I feel that I would be out of place not to mention two members of the senior class who are not here today—Andrew Jackson and Robert Washington. I know that many of you still grieve and that many of you wish that there was something you might have been able to do to prevent their deaths. Please know that I understand your pain, and if you're ever in trouble, please don't be afraid to ask for help—from me, or any member of the staff. We walk our paths here together. Please take care of yourselves, and take care of each other."

The auditorium was absolutely silent. The ringing of the bell shattered the moment, but the students were subdued as they hurried to their classes. I turned to Rhonda as we walked out together. "I gotta give him credit. Mr. Hathaway tries to have both heart and soul. That's hard to find in a principal."

"You got that right. It gave me chills." Rhonda shuddered.

"I just hope we can slide through this year with our eyes closed."

"What did you think of his son, the college kid?" I asked casually. I didn't want Rhonda to think I was interested in the dude.

"That's no kid. Kids are what we see every day. That's a *man*. And a fine one at that!" Rhonda said as she was bumped by the backpack of a ninth grader. The halls were crowded with kids yelling to each other, pushing to get through, going two different directions, banging doors of lockers, stopping in groups to have conversations.

"The whole idea of passing classes in four minutes is nuts!" I grumbled as we made our way down the hall to our first class. "He *is* fine,"

I continued, reflecting on Jonathan Hathaway, "but something about him makes me uncomfortable. Maybe it's those golden eyes."

"It's those eyes that make him look so good!" Rhonda laughed. "Of course, who's looking? I got my Tyrone and he makes me sizzle. I don't need any golden-eyed college boys. What about you, Keisha? You interested?"

"No way!" I said forcefully. "After Andy, I don't even want to talk to any dudes. They just cause pain." I could feel myself starting to cry, but I forced the tears back.

"Take your time, Keisha," Rhonda told me gently. "The hurt will go away eventually. We all miss Andy—and Rob, too."

Just then we bumped into a student who was obviously lost. She had her schedule in her hand, and was looking from the paper to each doorway, obviously trying to find a classroom.

"Need some help?" I offered.

"Where is Room One-ninety-nine?" she asked in exasperation. "I figured out that the one hundreds are on the first floor, the two hundreds are on the second, which makes sense, I guess. So where did they hide Room One ninety nine?"

Rhonda and I laughed as we fell into step with the new girl. "You must be new here," Rhonda commented.

"You a junior?" I asked.

The girl, who was dressed in a dynamite white cotton pantsuit, looked like a model. Her rich ebony skin and hair were a striking contrast to the thin, light, breezy material. Me and Rhonda eyed her outfit with appreciation. We recognized good taste in clothes.

"No, actually, I'm a senior," she admitted with a sigh. "My mom died last year, and I've come to live with my dad and his new wife."

"Rough way to start your senior year," I told her.

"Yeah, but my dad is trying to make it easy for me. His wife isn't bad for a stepmother, and they understand that I need time to adjust. I used to visit them every summer, but living here instead of New York is going to take some getting used to."

"I've lived here all my life"—I laughed—"and I still haven't got used to it!"

"New York City?" Rhonda asked.

"Yeah, right in Manhattan."

"Here's Room One-ninety-nine," Rhonda said as they climbed the steps and turned to a hall on the second floor.

"It's on the second floor?"

"Nobody knows why. Maybe just to confuse new kids," Rhonda shrugged her shoulders. "What's your name?"

"I'm Jalani," the new girl replied.

"That's a pretty name," I remarked. "Sounds Indian or something."

"It's Nigerian—Ibo to be exact. My mother was from Nigeria. It means strong and mighty, but I don't feel very strong or mighty today. It's hot and confusing, I miss my friends, I miss New York, and I really miss my mom." I could tell she was trying not to cry.

I touched Jalani's arm. "I know where you're coming from. We know about pain around here."

"Jalani, why don't you come with me and Keisha to the mall after school? I've got to get some new shoes. My mother doesn't understand, but I have *nothing* to wear with that new blue outfit I got."

Jalani brightened up. "Now, shoes I understand! When we moved here, I packed six boxes just for shoes! My mom never understood either." She sighed.

The bell rang then, and me and Rhonda hurried down the hall. As Jalani slipped into Room 199, Rhonda yelled, "Meet us by the main office after school!"

By the end of the day, the temperature outside had soared to ninety-five degrees. Inside the school, despite the open windows and useless fans, the students sweltered through that first day. Classroom temperatures had to be well over one hundred degrees. The building was old and impossible to air-condition.

I was first to reach the main hall after school. I sat on a bench, exhausted from the heat and the routine of the day. Gerald strolled over and sat next to me. "Rough day?"

"Yeah, it's hot, and I feel so alone. I miss Andy. Remember last year when he hooked up the janitor's hose and soaked everybody as they came out?" Gerald smiled, remembering. "Then he pointed that hose up to the sky, and let the water fall down on him and everybody around him. We were dancing and screaming and then Mr. Hathaway came out."

"Andy almost got Hathaway wet, but he did have a *little* bit of sense!" Gerald chuckled.

"Luckily, somebody warned Andy that Hathaway was coming around the corner," I said.

"It was Leon Hawkins—that silly dude with the good voice."

"Oh yeah, I had choir with him last year." I said. "He's crazier than Andy was." I sighed. "We could use a little Andy right now. When will this feeling go away, Gerald?"

"It will always be there, Keisha, but you'll learn to lock it away. If you don't, you'll let the pain eat you up." Gerald was surprisingly understanding.

I gave Gerald a hug to thank him. We saw Angel in the crowd and waved to her.

Angel looked confused at first, then smiled as she realized she had found her way to the main hall and found her brother. Gerald whispered to me, "Speaking of pain eating you up, look at Angel. She's so thin. I worry about her."

"She's a dancer, Gerald. She's supposed to be thin. I wish I had her figure."

Angel wore pale pink shorts and a matching top. Her large almond-shaped eyes seemed to fill her small face. Her waist was tiny, her legs sturdy but thin. She walked like a dancer.

"How was your first day?" Gerald asked. I could tell that he was proud of her—she was pretty and dainty, and I knew he would demolish any dude who tried to hurt her.

"Really good," she said breathlessly. "I've got homework already."

"Did you find the cafeteria?" Gerald asked.

"Yeah, but it was too hot and crowded in there. I ate outside with Joyelle. And yes, Gerald, I ate all the lunch you fixed for me." Angel rolled her eyes at her brother.

"Even the four cookies?"

"I gave one to Joyelle. Was that okay?" she teased him.

Gerald just grunted and pretended not to care. I could tell he didn't think she was telling the truth, however.

"Do you and Joyelle have any classes together?" I asked.

"All except first and last bell," Angel answered. "I think that's why the day was fun. Poor kid—she's got last-bell gym. Here she comes."

Joyelle dragged her way through the crowd of kids rushing to leave the building to the bench and plopped down with a groan. Her hair, which had been neatly curled that morning, was a frazzled, fluffy mess. Her new linen slacks, which she had insisted on wearing, looked as if they had spent the day balled up in the bottom of her closet. She was wrinkled and sweaty.

"Are all the days like this?" she asked finally. They all laughed as I offered her a cold Pepsi. She gulped it gratefully.

"This was easy," I told her. "Tomorrow it's still going to be hot, but it's going to rain. You can be soaked and miserable outside, and hot and sweaty inside, because they close all the windows. Not a good hair day."

"Oh, my hair!" Joyelle moaned.

We laughed. We'd all been there. Rhonda and Jalani walked over to us then. In contrast to Joyelle, Jalani looked cool, sleek, and self-assured. Gerald, who had been teasing Joyelle, looked up with a start.

"Hey, Gerald, this is Jalani—new to the senior class this year," Rhonda said, noticing

44

Gerald's instant attention to the new girl.

"What's up?" he said, unable to take his eyes from her. "You're . . . uh . . . the best thing I've seen all day."

"Excuse me," I interrupted. "You've seen me and Rhonda and a zillion other girls today."

"And I have *never* seen you quite so bold!" Rhonda added.

Gerald grinned, ignored us both, and tried not to show his nervousness. "Like I said, Jalani, you're the best thing I've seen all day."

She smiled and seemed pleased. "And that's the best line I've heard all day," she told him.

Angel asked, "Are you a model?" She seemed to be really taken with the smooth way Jalani moved and talked and dressed.

"I did quite a bit of modeling in New York," Jalani admitted. "It's fun, but really hard work."

Angel and Joyelle were impressed. "Have you been in any commercials?" Joyelle wanted to know.

"I do mostly print work. I've been in teen magazines and clothes catalogs. But you know that commercial for the hamburgers where the girl falls in love with the dude who sells the burgers?"

"That's you?" I shrieked. We were all impressed.

"I *knew* you looked familiar! Oh my gosh, you're famous!" Angel was jumping with excitement.

"Not really. But I made a lot of money. It's in a savings account for college. I'm going to major in fashion design."

"Wow!" Angel had a million questions. "Will you tell us about New York? How did you get started? How can I do that? Do we have any modeling agencies in Cincinnati?"

Jalani laughed. "It's nice to be treated like a celebrity, but I'm not one, really. And I promise, Angel, I'll answer all your questions. But right now, I'm going shopping with Rhonda and Keisha to get some shoes."

Angel and Joyelle nodded with excitement as they gathered their books to catch the bus home. Gerald had said very little, but he never took his eyes off Jalani. She glanced back at him as we left and smiled broadly. He smiled back, looking a little nervous. He looked like a kid who'd just discovered chocolate. Me and Rhonda cracked up as we headed with Jalani to my car.

I remembered much later that night, as I was reading chapter one in my world history book, that Jonathan Hathaway had been leaning against a far wall, watching us. I thought about it briefly, then fell asleep with my face in the book. History books do that to me.

4

The freshness of the first days of school faded quickly as September dragged on, hot and sticky. Class elections were held the third week of school, and I ran for senior class president against Elizabeth Espy, a pretty, popular cheerleader. I figured I didn't have a chance, but when the results were tallied, I was elected president; Elizabeth, as runner-up, was named vice president; Marcus Blake was elected secretary; and B. J. was elected treasurer, because everybody knew he could be trusted. I instituted a senior countdown calendar in the main hall, so we could all watch our days as high school students disappear. But the days seemed to move slowly in the warm weather, and homework kicked our butts every night.

One evening after school I went to the library to work on a report for English. I had my drugstore reading glasses perched on the end of my nose, two stacks of books to my right, a stack of notebooks to my left, and the slowest computer in the world in front of me. I sighed in frustration as I waited for the screen to rumble through the files to find the Web site that I was looking for. I had started looking for some information on *Beowulf* for English class. I ended up with more information than I needed, with pages on monsters and dragons and heroes. All I was trying to find was something about women of the time, but either there was very little information or women did very little during the seventh century in England.

The closest thing I found was a site about the mother of the monster in *Beowulf*, who was a woman—but a really ugly, stinky one, I noticed, who killed all the men in the countryside. That wasn't exactly what I was looking for. I sighed again, and tried once more. The screen listing was for something called "Boudica." "Who or what was a Boudica?" I wondered out loud. The computer whirred and began to spit out pages of information. "Hey now!" I almost yelled. The librarian looked over with bespectacled disapproval. I think they learn that in librarian school.

Jalani typed at the computer next to me. Jalani, who had decided to do her research on fashions of the dark ages, had gotten sidetracked, and was deep into a Web site that listed the words to the latest rap songs.

"You find anything?" Jalani asked. "This stuff makes me sleepy."

"Rap music makes you sleepy?" I asked as I glanced at Jalani's screen.

"No, these cultural connections Mrs. Blackwell wants us to make. I thought this was an English class. Why do we have to do all this history?"

"Must be some connection to us today," I mused. "But I haven't found it yet. I feel sorry for the people who lived back then."

"Why?" asked Jalani. "Because their lives were boring?"

"Because they had no toilets. No toilet paper. No microwave chili dogs!"

"I feel you. Have you seen the clothes they wore back then?" Jalani asked with amazement. "Unless you were rich, you wore long, ugly dresses and worked all day in the fields. It must have been rough being a girl during that time," Jalani said.

"But I found one woman who made a difference, at least for a little while," I told her.

"Who? A queen?"

"Not really. Her name was Boudica. She

was a princess of . . . let's see what it says here . . . some tribe called the Iceni, way back in A.D. sixty-one."

"Too long ago for me to care," Jalani said.

"No, this woman was really pretty cool," I tried to explain. "Even though her mama was stupid enough to give her a dumb name like Boudica!" We both laughed.

"Hey, what's up, my name is Boudica!" Jalani couldn't stop laughing.

"She sure wouldn't have made it in *our* school," I agreed, giggling at the image of a girl having to live with a name like that. "Anyway, she had long, flowing red hair down to her knees, with a deep voice and a huge body. She was over six feet tall and could beat up a man!"

"With a name like Boudica, she probably had to beat up everybody!" Jalani still couldn't stop laughing.

"She was a woman who could kick some butt if she really had to. And she had to."

"What happened?" Jalani asked, intrigued, wiping her eyes.

"When the Romans came to England to take over her people, they took her captive, beat her up, and raped her two daughters."

"Raped?"

"Yeah. Raped." I shuddered. Our laughter had died suddenly.

"Anyway, when they released the

50

women, Boudica was so angry that she went around the countryside, gathered up both men and women, and formed a little army all her own."

"You go, girl," Jalani said. "So did she chase the Romans out?"

I sighed. "She killed hundreds of them!" Me and Jalani smacked hands in a high five to celebrate Boudica's brief victory. "The fight lasted for almost a year, it says here. Then the Romans, of course, killed her."

"Of course." Jalani sighed.

"But for one brief moment in history, she showed the men what power really was," I said proudly.

"Is that who you're doing your report on?" asked Jalani.

"Yeah, there's no other woman who stands out like that for several centuries."

"I'm sure they existed. But nobody wrote about them in the books."

"Because the writers were all men!"

Jalani sighed again and turned back to her computer screen. "Okay, I'm inspired now. Let me find something as cool as you did. I'm going to download one of these pictures and see if I can make a sample dress like it. That way I can do my homework and learn a new design, too!" She went back to the screen cheerfully, printed out what she needed and, pleased with her idea, started planning how she would present her findings to the class.

I downloaded all I could find on Boudica, printed it out, and stretched as I got ready to finish for the day. "Jalani, are you about ready?"

"Yeah, let's raise up. Let's get a pizza on the way home, bet?"

I told her that was cool, so the two of us headed out of the library, past the security bars and cameras. Jalani's pager tripped off the security alarms, and after getting it checked and having our backpacks double-checked by the security guard, we headed into the large revolving doors, giggling about our double trip around the circular doorway in the same compartment, when we noticed someone in the other revolving compartment.

It was Jonathan Hathaway. He smiled broadly and circled back around so that he was standing outside the library with us.

"Done with your homework, ladies?" he asked cheerfully.

"Just a little research for Mrs. Blackwell. Our idea of fun is going to a mall; her idea of fun is going to a library!" I noticed that he was walking with us as we headed for my car. "Weren't you going into the library as we were leaving?" I asked.

"I just have to pick up a book I have on

reserve," Jonathan answered quickly. "You don't mind if I walk you to your car, do you? It gets dark so early now, and I'd hate to see anything happen to either of you."

"That's sweet of you, Mr. Hathaway," Jalani said. "It's hard to find someone who knows how to treat a lady these days."

"That's 'cause all the dudes we know are just boys!" I said with a laugh. "They need to take lessons from you, Mr. Hathaway," I teased.

"Please call me Jonathan," he said smoothly. "I'm not a real teacher yet. Just think of me as a friend from college—a friend who might like to get to know you better," he said, looking directly at me.

He made me feel funny when he looked at me like that. So I just said, "No, I'm not on that right now. I've got enough to do with homework and studying for the SAT and getting into college."

"I'm willing to help you with whatever you'd like," Jonathan continued, insistent. "I've got some SAT preparation study guides you can borrow, and if there's anything you'd like to know about college life, I'm your man!"

I looked up at him oddly as we got to my car. "I appreciate your offer, Mr. . . . uh . . . Jonathan, but I'd like to do this myself. You understand how it is, don't you?"

"Of course," he said in his smooth, mellow voice. "Just remember that I'm at your service. Any time. Twenty-four/seven." With that he turned and headed down the street. He did not go back in the direction of the library.

Me and Jalani got into the car and looked at each other in amazement. Then we cracked up with laughter.

"At your service. Twenty-four/seven." I made my voice deep and smooth.

"I'm your man!" Jalani laughed so hard she had to hold her sides.

"Whenever you need a voice made of butter and a line made of maple syrup, just call me!" I could barely breathe I was laughing so hard. Tears streamed down my cheeks. Jalani joined me as we continued to make fun of Jonathan Hathaway.

I started the car and we giggled about Jonathan Hathaway all the way home. When she got home, Jalani called Rhonda, who called me, who called Jalani again, and the three of us had another good laugh at his expense.

However, just before I fell asleep, I wondered for a moment how Jonathan just happened to be at the door as we were leaving. And I couldn't remember if he had gone back into the library after he walked us to the car or not. I shrugged and fluffed my pillow the way I liked it. All thoughts of Jonathan Hathaway passed as fatigue took over and I thankfully cuddled beneath the covers and slept.

5

October dawned golden, bright, and cool, a pleasant relief from all that heat we'd had in September. I like to watch the leaves fall when the breezes blow, and I love to run. I was on the cross-country team last season, but I didn't feel like competing this year, so I just practiced with the team to keep in shape. I don't do meets anymore—I run to please myself. I run for the freedom it gives me, for the release from memories that stab me in the gut, and for the way it makes my body feel strong and tight. Most coaches have told me that I'm a natural, smooth runner—I find energy instead of losing it as I run.

One cool October afternoon, I was jogging well—just listening to the rhythm of my shoes on the dirt path. It was about five o'clock, and already it was getting dark. I liked to run just a little ahead of most of the girls on the cross-country team, and a little behind the boys on the team.

The boys'-cross-country runners had already galloped past me that day, loping easily up the slopes and valleys of the park. Running in groups of two or three, they nodded at me as they ran. They were strong, muscular runners, with long legs and powerful lungs—most of them, at least. I giggled as I thought about B. J. He ran on the team as well. He wasn't tall and thin like the other runners, but his short legs were strong and he never seemed to tire. He grinned at me, taking time to run two circles around me before continuing with the group.

Leon ran with the team also. He was a solid runner, never flashy, but we could always depend on him to give the team what we needed to make a good showing at an event. He showed up just after B. J. I almost lost my stride, laughing at his silly outfit. He had on green trunks, a T-shirt that read "County Jail Escapee," and a Mickey Mouse hat on his head—his lucky running hat, he called it. Whenever the team went out for pizza after practice, Leon could be depended on to keep us laughing, putting breadsticks in his ears, burping Pepsi through his nose, and singing to the other customers in the restaurant. Afterward, we all went our separate ways. Leon always went home alone, not like some of the other kids on the team who hung out at each other's houses. I asked him about it one day as we were finishing practice.

"Hey, Leon. How come you never hang with the rest of the dudes?"

"No reason, really. It's always been that way. No big deal."

I hadn't pushed, but I could see in his face that it bothered him. "You like running?" I had asked, changing the subject.

Leon took a deep breath and smiled at me broadly. "Oh yeah!" he said with feeling. "I like cross-country because we run for long stretches—gives me time to think and breathe."

"I feel you," I replied. "I don't like sprints—too much effort and too little thought!"

Leon had laughed. "I also like being outside, even on rainy days. I like the smell of the trees and the dirt." He looked embarrassed all of a sudden—as if he had said too much.

"You can smell dirt? You got talents I never knew!" I teased him as I tossed my shoes into my gym bag. "I'm not that gifted, but I do like the way the wind makes me feel strong and powerful."

Leon had looked at me and hesitated before he said, "Me, too. At school I hardly ever feel that way." He had rushed off to his car then. I waved good-bye as he drove off, but he pretended he didn't see.

I slowed my pace a little and let the girls' team pass me as they thundered after the boys' team. They reminded me of long-legged Amazon warriors chasing their male captives. They ran easily, as if the brisk weather and the crispy leaves were created just for them.

I noticed Joyelle next. She was struggling a little, breathing harder and running slower than the others, but you gotta give it to her—she didn't give up. I shouted a couple of good words to her as she ran: "You go, girl!" Joyelle looked up and smiled at me with appreciation. She didn't run with the ease of the older girls who were in better shape. She had eaten far too many hamburgers and french fries to run with any speed or consistency. But she refused to give up, and she told me not long ago that in just the few weeks she had been running with us, she felt better, and her jeans zipped up a lot easier.

Just behind the girls' team jogged Jonathan Hathaway. I didn't notice at first when he started running next to me. My mind was on the colors of the leaves and how Andy had loved to rake a big pile of leaves, then jump into them. Jonathan was dressed in a silk—yes, silk—University of Cincinnati track suit, and he ran easily in and among the girls, encouraging them, handing out water, jogging easily at the pace he set for them. I watched as they looked at him—kinda like puppies at a kennel. They'd do anything to please him. If he smiled and winked a golden eye at one of them, she ran harder, striving to please him. Not me, though. Basically, I tried to ignore him. I slowed down and let the group get far ahead of me. Jonathan glanced back at me, but said nothing. He ran on with the girls' team. I finally slowed my pace to a walk, taking slow, deep breaths.

"Keisha! What are you doing out here?" It was Rhonda and Tyrone, their shoes shuffling through the crunchy leaves, holding hands.

"I run with the cross-country team a couple of times a week, remember?" I replied, as I bent over to stretch my leg muscles.

"Oh, yeah, that's right. Girl, when I get with Tyrone, I forget everything!"

"That's 'cause I'm such a powerful, potent dude!" Tyrone boasted, flexing his muscles like a bodybuilder.

"You talking about body odor or personality?" I asked him, laughing. Tyrone pretended to be offended. "What are you two up to?"

"Just walkin' and talkin'," Rhonda said quietly. "'Bout college and stuff." They fell into step with me as I walked back toward the parking area where the team bus was parked. Rhonda sighed. "You know, Keisha, in just a few months, me and Tyrone might be apart for years."

"It's not like we're going to prison—we're going to college," Tyrone reasoned. "Besides, there will be lots of vacations and breaks that we can be together. Tell her, Keisha."

"I'm not gonna get in the middle of this," I warned them, laughing.

"Do you think it's a good idea that me and Tyrone go to different colleges, Keisha?" Rhonda asked.

"I don't know. Probably. If your relationship is tight, it will last," I said, kicking the leaves. "Doesn't much matter what I think anyway. You two have got to figure out that stuff for yourselves."

"I got dreams, Rhonda," Tyrone said, looking directly at her and ignoring me.

"Me, too, Tyrone," Rhonda said quietly.

"Look, you two are crazy about each other. Don't sweat it!" I interrupted. "I gotta catch up with the team before the bus leaves me. Rhonda, call me tonight."

I sped up and left them in the leaves. I felt uncomfortable trying to help them figure out something they had to deal with themselves, and it made me mad that I had nobody to worry about being separated from. I just sighed and ran on.

When I got back to the bus area, most of the team was circled around Rita Bronson and Coach Jonathan Hathaway. Trying to figure out what was going on, I wedged my way into the group. Rita, one of the strongest runners on the team, was crying, and her sweats were all dirty and covered with leaves. One arm was bleeding, her neck showed a recent cut, and she was fiery-hot with anger.

Jonathan was saying, "Rita, if you'd get to practice on time, you wouldn't get lost and get yourself all bruised from falling in the bushes."

Rita's eyes were slits of knife blades. "I hope you choke on your own spit!" She pushed through the group and ran up the hill away from the bus.

"We'll discuss this later!" Jonathan yelled.

Rita tossed a couple of choice obscenities over her shoulder and continued to run toward the darkness of the woods.

"You come back here!" he shouted. She ignored him and ran faster, disappearing into the woods. Trying to save face and not look quite so blown away, Jonathan cleared his throat and announced, "We'd better go find her." He sent everyone out in groups of three, but Rita was nowhere to be found.

He took us all back to the school then, and filed a report about the "incident," as he called it, including Rita's disappearance into the woods. He tried to call her home several times, but no one answered. The whole scene was pretty weird.

When I finally got home, I was really tired, and a little concerned about Rita. She and I had never been close, but I knew something more than being late to practice had led to Rita's anger and disappearance. Rita was a senior—a strong runner, but she had often been in trouble at school. She used to cut class, she cussed out a teacher once, and she'd fight if you looked at her sideways. She once had a boyfriend who was almost thirty. We heard she would sneak out of her house to see him until her mother found out and threatened to have the man arrested. But lately, Rita seemed to have been trying to turn things around. She loved running cross-country and had helped the team win several meets.

I took a long, hot shower and arranged myself on my bed to study with a sandwich, a can of iced tea, and my physics book. Rita's problems faded from my mind.

Just as I opened my book, the phone rang. It was Rhonda. "What you doin', girl?"

"Tryin' to study for this physics test. You and Tyrone got it together yet?"

"Hey, that's why I called. He is *sooo* sweet!"

"Like candy, huh?"

"I just want to eat him up! Let me tell you what happened after you left."

"Spill it, girl." I closed my book and smiled at the excitement in Rhonda's voice. I knew this was gonna be good.

"Well, first he tells me that I am his dream, that without me he has nothing!"

"I always wanted a dude to tell me that— and really mean it," I told her.

"The air was smellin' good and the colors were all bright and I felt like I was in one of those movies where the music plays violins and stuff while the lovers walk through the forest."

"Cool. So it's really love, Rhonda?" I asked her seriously.

"You know, I'm not sure if love is like they make it look in the movies; but if love is feeling happy and at peace when he's around, and excited when I watch him walk across a room, and weak when he kisses me, then I'm in love for sure." She paused for a bit.

I asked her quietly, "So what happens now—that you're sure?"

Rhonda sighed. "I don't know, Keisha. I know I don't trust myself with him alone after dark. Because when I'm alone with him, I got no control. His kisses make me forget everything I ever believed in."

"What about him?" I asked, even though I knew the answer.

"He feels the same way. Maybe stronger. He kissed me while I was leaning against a tree and it was like a whirlwind began. My heart was pounding, my legs felt rubbery, and my entire body felt all squishy."

"Then what happened?" I asked. I knew Rhonda was going to tell me every detail whether I wanted to hear it or not.

"I reached up and touched his lips. Girl, so soft and delicious, those lips of his! Goodness! Then he kissed me again, and asked me what I was thinking. I didn't ask him. I *knew* what was on *his* mind!" Rhonda laughed.

"So what did you tell him?"

"I said, 'Tyrone, I want to tell you this in the daytime, while the sun is shining,' and he says, 'Well you better hurry—it's getting dark.' Then he unzips his jacket and pulls me closer to him and asks me real tender, 'What's wrong, Rhonda?' It was all I could do not to melt into caramel candy right there in his arms."

"Girl, this is heavy. Go on," I said.

"Well, I took a deep breath and I told

him, 'Tyrone, I don't want to be like some of the girls at school—like most of them, actually. I don't want to have sex just to see what it's like, or to get pregnant because the dude makes pretty babies, or to keep a count of how many dudes I can sleep with before graduation.' I said it real fast so I wouldn't lose my nerve."

"What did he say?"

"He told me he'd hate to think about me with anybody, except him."

"Well, that's good, isn't it?" I asked.

"Yeah, but he had to understand. So I told him, 'I know, but it's you and me I'm talking about. You make me want you, Tyrone, but I want to wait. Do you understand?'"

"I know lots of dudes who drop a girl when they say that and mean it," I told her. "What did Tyrone say?"

"He told me he loved me, Keisha! He says, 'I love you, Rhonda. I'm not just saying that because that's what a dude says to a girl. I really do care about every fuzzy little hair on your head.'"

"He's got you there!" I laughed. Rhonda's hair had been hard to handle since first grade.

Rhonda continued, "So he says, 'I don't want to do anything we're not ready for. What the dudes say about their women in the locker room is not where I want to be with you.' He told me he liked me long before he loved me, and because I was his friend as well as his girlfriend, he didn't want to do anything that would mess up our friendship. Is that amazing or what?"

"You got quite a dude there, Rhonda. Hang tight to that one!" I said with envy.

"Don't you worry!" Rhonda laughed with delight. "How was practice?" she asked.

"Interesting. Rob's little sister Joyelle is running with the team this year. She's not very fast, but she's got a lot of spunk, that kid. Rob would be proud of her."

"You're right. She's doing her best to make it this year," Rhonda said with admiration. "How's that fine young Hathaway doing as coach?"

"He's a good coach, I guess," I said. "He takes a lot of time with the girls."

"Yeah, I bet." I knew Rhonda was making a face on the other end of the line. "The girls follow him like flies around dead meat."

"Except for Rita Bronson," I added, remembering.

"Strange you should mention her," Rhonda said. "Me and Tyrone took her home tonight."

"Really? She was really upset at practice, and never did get on the bus. What did she say to you and Tyrone?"

"Well, we were heading back to Tyrone's car, and we saw something move in the distance. It was Rita—huddled in the dirt and crying. Her right arm was bleeding a little. So I asked her how she hurt herself. She seemed to be glad to see me, but all she would tell me is that she fell in some bushes and cut herself."

"I wonder what happened?"

"Maybe she's got home problems."

"I can feel that," I replied. "But she wouldn't say. I know she got yelled at by Coach Hathaway for being late to practice, and she was so angry that she tossed a couple of choice cuss words back in his face, telling him to stick his head where the sun don't shine!"

Rhonda hooted with delight. "Sweet! I bet that was worth hearing!"

"Then she just stormed off into the woods by herself. We couldn't find her after that. Jonathan and Leon looked for her for over an hour."

"So now he's *Jonathan*?" Rhonda interrupted me, laughing with delight. It was too good to slip by her unnoticed.

"That's what he told me to call him—all of us," I added quickly. I didn't want her to get the wrong idea. Rhonda said nothing, but I knew she was smiling on the other end of the phone. "So what else happened when you and Tyrone found her?" I asked, trying to change the subject.

"Well, Tyrone asked her if she wanted us to find Coach Hathaway, and she screamed *no!* like he had mentioned some serial killer," Rhonda said. "Then she told us that she had quit the team and refused to go back on the bus with them."

"I wonder what's going on," I mused. "I know she hangs with some pretty rough dudes sometimes."

"I don't know. She wouldn't talk about it," Rhonda said quietly. "She had a cut on her neck and her arm—looked like more than scratches from bushes to me. Then she asked us to take her home. She didn't say nothing in the car, but she thanked us and told us she'd see us on Monday."

"I wonder how much Coach Jonathan Hathaway knows about her situation. She seemed really angry at him—for more than just yelling at her about practice."

Rhonda thought about Coach Hathaway for a moment. "Keisha," she asked, "Jonathan is always dressed *so* fine! He's always walking around raggin' tough like he's got mass loot. Where do you think he gets the money? His dad?"

"I'm not sure," I replied, "but you're right about his threads. Hey, I gotta go. I'm gonna be too sleepy to study for this test." I hung up then, and wondered about the evening's events as I finished my homework.

Rita never came back to school. At first the story was that she was sick, then everyone figured she was just skipping school, or maybe had moved. School officials couldn't find her—letters to her mother came back unopened, the phone was disconnected, and no one answered at the door of the last address anyone had for her. Gradually she moved out of almost everyone's memory.

6

Angel was as thin as the sleet that fell most of
November. I noticed at school how thin Angel
was getting, but I barely had time to think
about it. I was busy with a part-time job at the
mall, mass homework, meeting with the other
class officers to plan for senior stuff, and
trying to figure out all the college material
that came in the mail. One Saturday afternoon
I ran into Gerald and Angel at the mall. Gerald
said he was on his way with Angel to take her
to dance class and they were headed to the
food court to get a bite to eat.

"What's up, Keisha?" Angel smiled
broadly. I think she kinda looked up to
me because I was a big-time senior who
looked like I had it together. Poor kid. If

71

she only knew how confused I felt.

"Not much. I'm on break from my job—which I'm gonna be quitting soon."

"How come?" asked Gerald.

"I've just got too much to do. I gotta keep my grades up—at least till I get accepted into college somewhere."

"Aw, Keisha, if your grades ever dipped down like mine do, you'd probably have a heart attack!" Gerald teased me. "Come with me and Angel. I'm gonna *watch* her eat this time!" Angel simply rolled her eyes at him and ordered a salad.

"Don't you want something else?" I asked Angel.

"We ordered pizza after practice this morning," Angel said, but her face said she was lying. "I'm stuffed." Gerald said nothing, but eyed her suspiciously as he ordered a cheeseburger.

"Dancing twice a day? Isn't that a bit much?" Gerald asked her.

"I'm just trying to get ready for our show. I have a chance for the lead!" Angel's eyes glowed with excitement and Gerald couldn't argue with her passion for her dancing.

I smiled at her as I ordered chicken, chips, and soup and we found a table. "Here, Angel, you can have my soup," I offered, placing it on Angel's tray.

"Thanks, Keisha," she said, "but I doubt if

I have room for so much food. Have you called Jalani yet?" Angel asked her brother, trying to change the subject. I grinned as we watched Gerald squirm. She knew he liked Jalani—everybody knew it, but he had yet to figure out how to tell Jalani himself.

"No," Gerald sighed. "What would a classy girl like Jalani want with a guy like me? I got nothing to offer. She's beautiful, she's got money, she's almost famous. She even drives a nicer car than I do. I just like looking at her. I wouldn't embarrass her by trying to talk to her. What would I talk about?"

"Give it a chance, Gerald. She told me she thinks you're cute!" I added, enjoying this too much.

"You're dumb, Gerald," Angel said as she nibbled at her salad. "You've got more class than most of the dudes in that school who are always hanging around her. She knows a real man when she sees one. Have you noticed that she doesn't talk to any of them?"

"She's right, Gerald," I told him, taking one of his french fries.

"Well, if she doesn't want to talk to any of them, I know she doesn't want to talk to me!"

"Maybe she isn't talking to them because she'd rather be talking to you," reasoned Angel.

"Not a chance!"

"Give it a try."

"Can't." I know Gerald hated feeling like a seventh-grade idiot, but that was how Jalani affected him.

"Like I said, dumb!" Angel repeated. "But I love you, Gerald. You just have to believe that you're lovable."

"You have to love me 'cause I'm your brother."

"I have to love you because you have a car now and I have a ride home, even if it is an old beat-up Ford!"

"She has a new red BMW!" I added.

"Don't remind me!" groaned Gerald.

"So ask her for a ride in it." Now I knew that Jalani would jump at the chance to talk to Gerald, but she had too much dignity to call him first.

"Not a chance," Gerald insisted.

"Give it a try."

"Can't."

"Like I said, dumb!"

"Talk about dumb! You ate nothing! Here, finish my fries—the ones that Keisha didn't sneak off the plate!"

"I hate cold fries—and I told you I ate after practice." Angel got up from the table and put on her coat. Her large down coat made her tiny body look even smaller. "See ya, Keisha. We tried to talk some sense into his big head!"

I watched them leave and thought about

Gerald's pride. He and Angel lived in a high-rise apartment in a low-rent neighborhood. I knew that Gerald wasn't ashamed of where he lived, but he had told me many times that he was afraid that a girl who had modeled in New York and drove her own red BMW wouldn't understand the world that Gerald called home. And he wasn't going to give her the chance to find out. I sighed and headed back to my job.

After work, while I was unlocking the door to my house, I could hear the phone ringing insistently. I dropped my purse and packages, and chuckled at myself. What was I working for? More than half of my paycheck went for clothes at the store I worked at! Even with my employee discount, I had very little left. But I did get to rag it tough! I rushed to pick up the phone. It was Jalani, sounding concerned.

"What's wrong?" I asked.

"It's Angel!" Jalani told me breathlessly. "She collapsed at dance class tonight and had to be rushed to the hospital!"

"Oh no! I just saw Angel and Gerald at the mall a few hours ago! Were you there when it happened? Tell me what's goin' on!"

"I started taking classes at the conservatory a few weeks ago," Jalani explained. "I didn't even know Angel was taking classes there, too. But right in the middle of class, a girl ran into our room, screaming, 'Help! Somebody call Nine-One-One! A girl passed out in our class!' So I ran over there to see if I could help, and it's Angel sprawled out on the floor. It was scary."

"So what did you do?" I asked. My heart was pounding.

"Well, Angel's teacher's got gumdrops for brains. She's screaming hysterically into the confusion, 'Does anyone know CPR?'"

"You mean the dance teacher didn't know CPR? That's unbelievable!"

"That's what I thought, but I didn't have time to worry about her problems just then. Angel didn't look like she was breathing. So I told the ditzy teacher that I knew CPR, and me and this other girl in my class started doing the breathing and compressions."

"So was Angel breathing at this point?" I interrupted.

"I don't know, girl. Angel didn't move, except for the movements we made as we worked on her. I was so scared we were going to lose her. She was blue and clammy, and so thin and frail. Pretty soon we heard the sirens from the life squad. I just prayed they'd get there in time."

"Oh my goodness! What happened when they got there? Did she come to?"

"Hold on. I'm trying to tell you. When the life squad burst in the door, Gerald was right behind them, screaming her name. He'd been waiting in the parking lot, and when he saw the ambulance, he told me later that somehow he just knew it was Angel they had come for. That dude really loves his baby sister!"

"You got that right! So tell me, what happened then?"

"Gerald ran to the front, pushing the paramedics aside, screaming, 'That's my sister!' They got him out of the way by explaining that he was stopping them from helping her, so he just stood there helplessly, not ashamed to cry or pray."

"Poor Gerald," I murmured. "I feel for him."

"While they worked on her, setting up oxygen and starting an IV and stuff, I walked over to Gerald and took his hand. It was as natural and easy as breathing. He was so scared. He grabbed my hand, forgot about how scared he was of me, and didn't turn it loose until they took Angel out of there. I don't think he was even aware of it. He was only thinking about Angel."

"So when they took her out, was she breathing?"

"Yeah, her color had returned just a little and her eyelids had flickered a little. The paramedics told Gerald they had her stabilized and for him to follow them to the hospital. He was too shaky to drive, so we ended up going in my car."

"It's funny how things happen," I told her.

"Gerald has been dying to talk to you and ride in your BMW, and all of a sudden, because of a crisis, it falls in his lap."

"I know. If both of us hadn't been so scared of what might happen to Angel, it might have taken the whole school year before he got around to talkin' to me." Jalani chuckled. "The paramedics said before they pulled out, 'Angel is in good hands now. You two drive carefully. I don't want you and your girlfriend getting hurt.' Gerald and I both giggled a little over that," Jalani admitted.

I still sat on the floor among the bags I had brought in with me. I had taken off my coat and shoes and listened like no tomorrow. "I feel you, girlfriend."

"It was cold out there, and all I had on was my leotard, so Gerald gave me his jacket. It smelled like him—kinda warm and leathery." Jalani stopped for a moment, remembering.

"What happened when you got to the hospital?" I asked softly.

"Oh, Gerald tried to reach his mother, but she wasn't home and not at work, so he dealt with the questions and the paperwork by himself. There was nothing else to do but wait. So he paced. He bit his fingernails. He prayed. I wasn't sure what to do. Finally he told me, 'I don't like this place.'"

I told Jalani, "There's a good reason for that. That's the hospital where they took

Robbie after the accident, and where they took Angel after the fire in their apartment. Also, I think an aunt he used to live with was taken there when she died. It's no wonder the place freaks him out."

"He told me a lot of that while we waited. I took his hand and asked him to tell me all about Angel. That helped—he enjoys talking about her. I had no idea what troubles they've lived through. He told me about how he first found out he had a sister, how he loved her and protected her. He told me about how he found out that she was being abused by their stepfather, and about the fire that had saved them both. When he had finished, I think he felt better. He told me I was easy to talk to."

"Gerald is solid," I said. "Built tough."

"I'm starting to see that," Jalani said with admiration in her voice. "Then he asked me to tell him about my life, about how I ended up going to Hazelwood in my senior year and why I gave up modeling in New York. So I told him everything. He was so easy to talk to."

"I don't think you've ever even told me and Rhonda more than bits and pieces," I said.

"I know. It's hard being new among so many old friends. I was a little scared at first, but now I feel closer to all of you," Jalani said quietly. "I know Gerald thought I'm all that because I have a nice car and such, but my life has been rough, too," she began. "I was born in Nigeria. My mother was Nigerian, an Ibo, and my father an American missionary. We lived in a village out in the bush, with dirt floors, no windows, and no toilet. But I was happy as a child because my mother loved me, my father spoiled me, and I had the love of the whole village, who all treated me as if I were their own."

"I bet that was awesome," I said.

"When hard times came because of the droughts and political problems," she continued, "my parents decided to move back to the States. We lived in shacks and tenements all over the South while my father preached. But gradually, my mother got tired of his refusal to settle down, and of his frequent descents into what he called 'forgivable sin.' Mother got tired of forgiving him for giving more than brotherly love to the women in the congregation, so they split up. It broke her heart, but it made her stronger."

"Rough stuff," I told her. "So that's when you went to New York?"

"Yeah. Mother and I found a small place of our own right in the middle of New York City. She loved the fast pace of the place. I started modeling when I was very young, and she never let me spend a penny of it. She saved it, learned to invest it, and tripled what I had in five years, then tripled that amount in the next two years. It's almost as if she knew I would need something to survive on."

"So that's how you saved enough for the BMW?" I asked, interrupting.

"Goodness, no. Mother would never have let me spend that much on a car. She won it on *Wheel of Fortune!* It was the most fun she ever had in her life." Jalani grew silent on the other end of the line. "I guess I told you that mother was diagnosed with cancer two years ago, and she gradually faded away into darkness. I thought that I couldn't live when she died last year. Gerald was so understanding when I told him."

"I told you he was an awesome dude. Now all this is happening while you're waiting to find out about Angel?"

"Yeah, the waiting was the worst part— the not knowing. Being able to talk to each other really helped. I told him he was very strong. In my home village the men would have said that he had been through the fire and the scars had made him a strong and mighty man."

"Now I never quite thought of him as mighty," I said, laughing, "but he has had his share of tough luck."

"By that time, a doctor came out and called for Gerald. He grabbed my hand and we walked over there together."

"What did the doctor say? Is Angel going

to be okay?" I asked with worry, remembering the reason for Jalani's call in the first place.

"She told Gerald that Angel was seriously dehydrated and anemic. The tests said she was downright malnourished. Then the doctor asked Gerald when was the last time that Angel had eaten a good meal."

"Oh, no! What did Gerald say?"

"He felt guilty, of course, like it was his fault that Angel wasn't eating. He told the doctor that Angel was a dancer who took pride in being thin and that she had been working real hard to get a part in a performance—dancing several hours a day—and eating very little. I tried to tell him that it wasn't his fault, but he was really upset."

"Did the doctor say what was wrong with Angel?"

"She said Angel's got anorexia nervosa and it's common in young dancers and gymnasts. These kids starve themselves to death, and they're not even aware that's what they're doing."

"That's deep—and scary, too."

"It's worse than that," Jalani said. "Gerald told me that Angel's dance teacher constantly called the girls fat and made fun of them for their size."

"You're lyin'!" I said with astonishment.

"No, I'm for real. The doctor didn't believe it either. Gerald said that Angel's teacher told them that only the thinnest and smallest girls got to be professionals in New York. The doctor just sighed and shook her head."

"So did they keep Angel at the hospital?"

"They're going to keep her overnight, feeding her with an IV and making sure her fluid levels are back to normal, but she'll be able to go home tomorrow," Jalani said.

"So what happens then? Is there a cure for anorexia?"

Jalani sighed. "The doctor told Gerald that first of all, obviously, Angel's gotta eat. Lots of tiny meals instead of three big meals. Lots of encouragement from all of us. Lots of support and understanding because when she looks in the mirror, she really does see a fat person. And she should probably see a nutritionist or somebody who specializes in anorexia. And if all this doesn't happen, the doctor said that Angel could die."

"Oh my." I was stunned into silence.

"I told Gerald I would help as much as I could," Jalani said. "So much has changed in just one night."

"I'm glad you were there for them tonight, Jalani," I told her.

"Me, too. I gotta go. I'm really sleepy."

"G'nite, Jalani."

"G'nite, Keisha."

7

December began with a blizzard. Fifteen
inches of snow covered Cincinnati like a thick,
white winter blanket, and the temperatures
dipped down to fifteen degrees. Schools, work
places, even the malls were closed. I love snow
days—no stress, no schedules, no homework.
On that cold December day, I hadn't even
gotten out of bed yet. I was cuddled under
tons of blankets, reading a book I had checked
out of the library. The phone rang and I waited
till the fourth or fifth ring to pick it up. "Hello."

I heard a male voice clear his throat. "May
I speak to Keisha please?"

"Speaking."

"This is Jonathan Hathaway. I hope I'm
not disturbing you."

I was mildly surprised that he was calling me. I had kept my distance during cross-country practice, and though I sensed that he was interested in me, he rarely said anything to me that was not related to running or training. He always smiled and was pleasant when I was around, and he went out of his way to say hello when I saw him in the halls at school. That was cool with me.

"No, I was just reading and enjoying this snowy day," I told him.

"Well, that's why I called, sort of." He hesitated. "I'm taking some students skiing this afternoon—mostly seniors and a couple of kids from the cross-country team. Just for a couple of hours up at Perfect North Slopes. Would you like to go?"

I was truly surprised. I thought about my warm bed and my good book and started to turn him down, but I loved skiing and didn't often get the chance. "Sure, why not? Sounds like fun."

I could hear him sigh with relief. "I'll pick you up in an hour if that's okay."

He hung up and I dragged myself out of bed to find my long underwear and heavy jacket. I called my mother at work, told her where I was going, and after listening to her warn me about frostbite and windburn, I fixed myself a cup of hot chocolate and got dressed. As I dug in my bottom drawer for my left glove, I called Rhonda, but there was no answer. So I called Jalani.

"What's up, girlfriend?" Jalani said.

"Not much. For sure not the temperature. I must be crazy to think about getting out of my nice warm bed out into that freezing wet stuff outside."

"So what's making you go?"

"Jonathan Hathaway called. He's taking some kids from school up to Perfect North Slopes to ski. I told him I'd go." I think I sounded as if I was having second thoughts.

"What's wrong with that? Beside the fact that you're gonna freeze your buns off, why not go? It's not like a date, you know."

"I never said anything about a date!" I said defensively. I don't know why that bothered me, but it did.

"You know he's got a thing for you," Jalani teased.

"I know somehow he always seems to be around. But he does seem nice," I admitted.

"And he is *so* fine!" Jalani reminded me.

"That has nothing to do with it. I'm going to make him stop by and pick up Monty also. Monty likes hanging around us, and he needs to laugh and have a little fun."

"So you're going out with Jonathan to help Monty."

"I am *not* going out with Jonathan!" I yelled into the phone. "He's just the driver."

"Sure, Keisha. Have fun." Jalani chuckled on the other end of the line. "I'm going over to Gerald's to see how Angel is doing. Call me when you get home."

Jonathan arrived, eyes bright with excitement. He thanked me for giving up my warm bed and walked me carefully over the ice and slippery snow to the driveway where Rhonda and Tyrone and B. J., along with Leon and Marcus from the team, sat waiting in the back of Jonathan's roomy Jeep Cherokee wagon. Jonathan wore a sky-blue down ski jacket with matching ski pants and hat, looking just like a model out of *GQ*, dressed for successful skiing, while the others wore an assortment of school jackets and probably a couple pairs of jeans. He checked the angle of his cap in the rearview mirror, adjusted it slightly, then pulled off into the snowy afternoon.

"I didn't know you guys were going," I said cheerfully.

"We didn't either," B. J. replied. "It just sounded like fun."

"Hey, Leon, good to see you! What's up?" I said casually.

"Chillin'!" Leon replied with a grin. Everyone laughed, especially since it was so cold outside. Leon reached into his pocket and pulled out a huge snowball. "Hey! This must be why my hands are so cold!"

"Leon, you're crazy!" I shouted. "Get that thing out of here!"

Leon replied with a grin, "As you wish, my lady!" He rolled the window down all the way, while everyone inside the car yelled at him for letting in that blast of freezing air, and tossed the snowball onto the road. I just shook my head, laughing and marveling at the silliness of high school boys.

"I tried to call you, Rhonda, but now I know why I got your mom's machine," I told her.

"B. J. called and told me that instead of sitting through another boring physics lecture, we could experience it firsthand!" Rhonda explained.

"The bell would be ringing right now," B. J. reminded them.

"And we would all lean over and get out our notebooks," I began, thankful we were sitting in a Jeep Cherokee, not a classroom.

"Mr. Simpson would start to talk," Rhonda continued.

"He'd turn on the overhead projector," B. J. said.

"He'd dim the lights," Leon added.

"Our eyes would glaze over," I said, as if in that trance.

"And Mr. Simpson would drone on about slopes and angles," Rhonda continued, giggling.

"And that would be just the first five minutes of class!" B. J. laughed triumphantly.

"Then Leon would walk in," I reminded them.

"Late, as usual," Tyrone added.

"Without his homework!" Rhonda continued.

"But with the best excuses in the world!" I added, laughing. "What was that long one you gave Mr. Boston last year?"

"I don't have my homework because I left it in my dad's truck," Leon started to say.

"'So bring it tomorrow,' the teacher says," B. J. continued, laughing as he remembered.

"And I say sweetly to old man Boston, 'I can't bring it tomorrow.'" Leon loved to drag a story out.

"'And why not?' old Boston says, with his high-water pants, bad teeth, and bad breath," B. J. added, continuing the suspense.

"Well, my dad is a long-distance truck driver, sir," Leon said, "and he's on his way to California! And he won't be back for three weeks! So I'll give you my homework next month! It's not my fault!"

Everyone in the car cracked up. It felt good to laugh.

"Did you call Gerald?" I asked Rhonda.

"Gerald wanted to stay home with Angel. She's really doing lots better," Rhonda reported happily. "And lately, Jalani stays pretty close to wherever Gerald happens to be."

I grinned. "I just talked to Jalani. That's where she was headed. I'm glad for them. Remember how scared he was of her?" I noticed that Leon had become unusually quiet.

B. J. added, "We've got one more stop. I thought it would be nice to ask Joyelle. With Angel sick, Joyelle is really lonely."

"That's nice of you, B. J.," I told him.

We pulled into Joyelle's driveway, and she waddled out to the car. Her mother had made her put on so many clothes, she could hardly walk. She climbed in the back and began to remove scarves and gloves and extra jackets, as everybody laughed. Joyelle knew better than to complain—her mother was extra sensitive to her daughter's health and safety since she had lost Rob.

"What about Monty?" I asked Jonathan. "Can we take one more?"

"Sure," he replied easily. "Use my cell phone and call his house." Monty, of course, was thrilled. He met the car in the driveway; his mother waved from the front door.

I sat in the front seat between Jonathan and B. J. I was conscious of my leg touching Jonathan's, but I couldn't squeeze very far away in the crowded car. The roads were surprisingly clear, for the salt trucks had been out all night. The sky was a vivid blue, and the snow-covered trees looked bright and shiny in the sunlight.

We pulled up to the lodge, piled out, and paid our fees and rented skis. Jonathan, of course, had his own skis, sleek and glossy in a custom case. As he reached down to snap them, I noticed that something tiny and metallic clinked to the tiled floor beneath his boots.

Now I'm a good skier, but this was my first time this winter, so I started on the gentler slopes. The air bit my face like tiny knives. I hated to admit it, but my mother, as usual, was right.

I took Monty down a small hill, called Little Bluff, and even though it was his first time on the slopes, he did well and didn't fall once. The expression on his face as he reached the bottom of the hill was worth the effort of getting him ready to do it. He was exultant. "Let's do it again!" he cried. So we took the lift back up. That's when B. J. offered to take him down another, bigger hill, so Monty left me in an instant, excitedly following B. J. I smiled as I watched him go. It was good to see him happy.

I saw Leon in the distance, and noticed he was heading my way, but just then, Jonathan skillfully skied over to where I stood. "Race you down!" he challenged, and I forgot all about Leon for the moment.

"You're on!" I answered Jonathan as I took off. He barely had time to put on his goggles before I had left him in a swirl of snow. He laughed as he took off behind me, easily catching and passing me.

"Good thing this was Little Bluff," I gasped. "I would have left you like yesterday's snowman."

"Are you ready for Deception Hill?" he asked. "I dare you to try."

I hesitated. Deception was steep and curved, and considered one of the most difficult hills on the slopes. "I tell you what," I offered, "instead of racing, let's just try skiing. I don't think I'm ready for racing on Deception yet."

"Good idea," he agreed. We skied together toward the chair lift that would take us to Deception, sliding easily in unison. I found on the ride that Jonathan was easy to talk to, and seemed to have been everywhere and done everything. He had skied in Switzerland, had taken hot-air balloon rides in Kenya, and had even been scuba diving in Australia. I chatted to him about my plans for medical school, my hopes of learning to fly a plane, and my worries about college.

When the lift dropped us off at the top of the slope, the view was breathtaking. It looked like one of those paint-by-number pictures that I used to do when I was ten years old.

Bright, clean snow covered the world—it looked like tons of spilled sugar. The pine trees decorated the scene with green. I breathed deeply of the cold, fresh air. It was the first time in several months that I had felt truly free.

"Thank you," I said suddenly to Jonathan.

"For what?" he answered in surprise.

"For making me get out of bed. For talking to me like I'm a person, not a kid. For bringing me to this beautiful place." I was silent for a moment. "I know we teased you that night at the library, but there really is a big difference between you and the high school boys I've known since kindergarten. I've never had a conversation like we just had. It was refreshing—just like this wind."

Jonathan grinned with pleasure. "You're so mature, Keisha. Maybe that's why the boys your age don't appeal to you."

"One of them did," I replied quietly. "But he's gone."

"I've heard all about Andy," Jonathan said carefully. "I'm really sorry, Keisha."

"Can we take the lift back down, Jonathan? I think I'd rather just talk a little more than try to prove to you I'm bad enough to try Deception. Besides, I'm cold."

"I was just going to suggest that. Let's find the others and head back home. Monty is probably an icicle by now."

I laughed as we got back in the lift. Deception could wait.

"Keisha," Jonathan said to me when we got back to the bottom of the hill, "I really enjoyed today. Would you like to go to the movies sometime? If you think it's not appropriate, just let me know."

I thought for a moment. Then I surprised myself and said, "I think I'd like that." He smiled with delight, but said nothing more as the others started to head toward us.

We gathered the rest of the group and headed back to Jonathan's wagon, tired and cold, but feeling really mellow. Monty fell asleep as soon as the car heater warmed up. The rest talked quietly about the hills and the spills of the day. Rhonda snuggled close to Tyrone. Joyelle nodded on Tyrone's other shoulder. B. J. glanced back at her and smiled. Leon looked quietly out of the window, watching the snow. Jonathan glanced at himself briefly in the rearview mirror, turned on a smooth jazz station, and we headed back to Cincinnati to the mellow sounds of the saxophone. For the first time in months, I felt like the rock where my feelings used to be was starting to dissolve. The snow had started to fall again.

8

The next day, school was once again cancelled because of the snow and the bitterly cold temperatures. I cheered sleepily when I heard the announcement on the radio, then went back to sleep with a pillow over my head. Jalani called a couple of hours later, waking me from a confusing dream about dolphins on a ski slope.

"You up, girl?"

"Do I have to be?"

"It's so pretty outside!"

"It'll still look good when I get up," I grumbled good-naturedly. "What's on your mind?"

"I'm on my way to see Angel. She needs lots of encouragement. Want to come with me?"

"Don't you mean you're on your way to see Gerald?" I teased her.

"I can't help it if he lives there!" Jalani laughed.

"You think the corner coffee shop is closed today?"

"No, those places never get days off for bad weather. I'd hate to work there."

"Okay. Buy me a cup of hot chocolate and a donut to warm me up, and I'll come with you," I said. I didn't want to stay home alone all day anyway. My parents, of course, had gone to work, grumbling about school kids who got to stay home and sleep in on snowy days.

"Bet. I'll see you in an hour or so."

I stretched, climbed out of bed, and looked outside. Every tree limb, telephone wire, lightpost, and street sign was covered with several inches of shining snow. I thought it looked as if one of those magic princesses from those old European folk tales had touched the city with a magic wand, turning everything to diamonds made of snow.

An hour later, I was in Jalani's car clutching a warm cup of hot chocolate, hoping the little BMW wouldn't slip on the icy roads. But Jalani drove carefully and pulled into a parking space that had been cleared of snow right in front of Gerald's apartment building.

"Grab that container of soup, would you,

Keisha," Jalani asked as she gathered up the bag of donuts and a windshield scraper.

"Got it!" I replied. We tiptoed up the unshoveled walkway, leaning on each other while trying not to fall. I glanced to my left, and noticed a woman huddled in a corner, near the heat exchange unit of the building. She had on several coats, a number of scarves, and two hats. One of her boots was red, the other was blue. She looked like she was either asleep or dead.

"Is it Christmas yet, chil'ren?" the woman asked, suddenly sitting up, startling us and making us gasp.

"Excuse me?" I said hesitantly.

The woman spoke louder this time. "Is it Christmas yet?"

"No, ma'am," I told her. "We've got three more weeks. Why do you ask?"

"'Cause at Christmas they give us food and clothes. Like we ain't hungry or cold any other time."

We weren't sure what to say. I don't think either of us had ever had a conversation with a homeless person before. "Would you like some soup?" Jalani asked the woman suddenly, taking the soup from me and offering it to the woman. "I made it myself."

"Hot soup?" the woman asked. She acted like Jalani was offering her a basket of diamonds or something.

"Yes, ma'am," Jalani replied.

"Girls like you can't cook. Your mama made it."

"My mama is dead. She taught me how to cook, though. It's Nigerian stew."

"I'm sorry, baby. Sorry 'bout your mama, too. Young people usually ain't very nice to me. I been beat up twice."

Again neither of us was sure what to say. "Do you want the soup, ma'am?" Jalani asked again.

"Yes, I would. Thank you, honey. And what you know about Nigeria? You from Africa?"

"Yes, ma'am. I was born there."

"Always wanted to see Africa," the old woman muttered to herself. "I guess talkin' to somebody who was born there is good enough!" Then she looked at me. "You from Africa, too, Miss Girlfriend?

"No, ma'am. I've never been very far from Cincinnati," I told her.

"Well get to Africa while you're young. Then you won't have to be wishin' when you get to be old like me. 'Sides, ain't no snow in Africa— leastways not the parts I'm dreaming of!"

I didn't want to offend her, so I just said, "Yes, ma'am."

The old woman looked up suddenly. "My name's not 'ma'am.' It's Edna." She chuckled. "Ain't that an ugly name?"

"I think it's a nice name," Jalani said. She

handed the whole bowl of soup in the plastic container to Edna, who gulped it greedily. She had no need of a spoon—she was very hungry.

"What's your name, honey?" Edna asked Jalani as she finished off the soup.

"Jalani."

"Now that's a pretty name!" Edna declared. "A nice African name! I like that! And you're a pretty girl to match it."

Jalani smiled shyly.

"And what's your name, chile?" she asked me. "I never said you was ugly, now. Don't go gettin' mad at ol' Edna." I smiled and told her my name.

"Keisha? What kind of name is that? Sounds like a sneeze!" She wiped her mouth on her coat sleeve and laughed at her own joke. I smiled, but I said nothing.

"Do you have someplace to go, Edna?" Jalani asked.

"Sure, chile. Don't you worry none about me. I'm heading down to the shelter for the night. I'll be fine. 'Specially now that I had that soup. The food they give us down there is clean and good, but it's made from what I call recycled leftovers, if you know what I mean. Nothing wrong with it; it just ain't fine cuisine, if you know what I mean. Not rich and fine like your homemade soup! I'll sleep good tonight, thanks to you!"

Jalani started to cry. "I wish I could help you," she mumbled helplessly.

"Now, child, ain't nobody cried about me in a hundred years or so. So don't start now. I like my life. I got no bills, no obligations, no worries. I got friends here on the streets and a warm place to sleep on these winter nights. And every once in a while, I meet a couple of kids like you that lets me know the world is gonna be okay. Now get on inside out of this cold. Both o' you! You done a good thing today. And that's just 'bout good enough!"

She handed Jalani the empty container and smiled at both of us. She was a large woman, and she stood up, stretched, and sort of waddled down the street toward the shelter. Me and Jalani stood there staring, not quite sure what to say or do. Edna glanced back at us, "Get out of the cold, chil'ren. Ol' Edna gonna sleep good tonight!" Edna turned the corner and disappeared into the snowy afternoon.

We slowly climbed the steps to Gerald's apartment and knocked on the door. Gerald opened it and grinned. He looked at Jalani the way Edna had looked at that soup, then glanced at the empty plastic soup container.

"Got hungry on the ride over?" he teased.

"I gave it to a homeless lady," Jalani said

slowly. "It was the strangest experience." We told Gerald and Angel about our encounter with Edna as we took off our coats and gloves.

Jalani fixed Angel a microwaved baked potato, decorated with cheese and bacon. We all watched Angel eat it slowly, teasing little bites into her until it was just about gone. It took almost an hour, so we played Scrabble while she ate.

"I know what you guys are trying to do," Angel said between bites. "You're trying to fatten me up so you can feed me to the wicked witch!"

"You've discovered my secret!" laughed Jalani with a screech. "I *am* the wicked witch! Eat that potato, my child. I need meat for my porridge!" We all laughed so hard we knocked the game board off the kitchen table.

Later, we sat in front of the TV, sharing a box of raisins, watching the weather reporters talk about the snow.

"My stomach hurts, Gerald," Angel complained. "It always hurts when I eat."

"Mine hurts when I *don't* eat," replied Gerald. "Your stomach hurts because it's not used to food."

"Food makes me sick," Angel whined.

"Food keeps you alive. You've got it backwards," Jalani told her patiently.

"Why do I have to eat so much? I'm already so fat!"

"You've had six raisins and you're *not* fat!" I told her.

"And a potato!" she wailed. "When I see myself, I see a huge, disgusting elephant," Angel explained. "I don't *want* to, but I can't help it!"

"I know, Angel," Gerald said gently. "But you are a lovely, slim, foxy lady. You gotta believe me. He grinned at her and tickled the bottom of her feet.

She giggled and jerked her knees up. He gave her two more raisins and she ate them, but real pain crossed her face as she swallowed. "It really does hurt, Gerald," she said seriously.

I tried a different approach. "Listen, Angel. Your body's running on empty. That's why it hurts. You have to put gas in so the car will run right. Here's some more gas," I teased, as I fed her more fruit.

"Do you think I still have the part in the show?" Angel asked us.

"When I talked to Mrs. Christoff last week, she said she was holding the part for you," Gerald told her, "but do you know what she told me?" Gerald shook his head in disbelief, remembering.

"What?" I asked.

"I tried to explain to her about the seriousness of anorexia and how we were going to take this very slowly, and she said, as if she was talking to some idiot who ought to know this, 'Oh, all the great dancers are anorexic! I've been anorexic all my life.' She said it with pride!"

"The woman is a walking box of Cracker Jacks," I said. I couldn't believe a grown-up in charge of kids could be so stupid.

I shuddered at the thought of Mrs. Christoff year after year preaching the gospel of anorexia to hundreds of unsuspecting kids like Angel.

Angel sighed in agreement. "I've heard her say that many times, and I just believed her. She danced with the New York City Ballet, you know."

"Yeah, I know, she told me," Gerald said. "I think the woman's got some issues that we don't need to deal with."

"Maybe we need to talk about this, Angel," Jalani said gently. "Maybe you should take a little break from ballet until you get your strength back." We waited for her reaction.

"Not dance?" Angel asked, her eyes getting wide and scared-looking. "Dancing is like breathing to me. You don't understand!"

"Not forever, Angel," Gerald added. "Just until summer. Maybe we can find another dance school. One where the teacher knows

CPR and lets you have water and doesn't tell you how big you are. Right after Christmas, we'll start looking for another place to dance. Bet?"

"Bet," Angel replied quietly. She smiled doubtfully, but stopped arguing.

Jalani and I left a couple of hours later. She probably would have stayed longer if I hadn't been with her. I sighed. I was getting tired of being the third wheel on all these two-wheeled couples.

There was no sign of Edna when we went outside, and Jalani told me later that even though Gerald looked for a homeless woman who fit Edna's description every morning when he left for school and every evening when he came home, he couldn't find her.

9

"You want to go out with who?" My mother had that look on her face—the one that's supposed to make you feel guilty, or sorry you asked the question.

"Jonathan Hathaway," I said for the tenth time.

"Absolutely not!" My dad's look was that protective-of-his-little-girl daddy look—it made you feel just as guilty, but not as mad as mom's look did. Daddy didn't think any human male would ever be good enough for me. And a twenty-three-year-old man was going to be out of the question.

I sighed with exasperation as I tried to explain. "He's the principal's son. How bad could he be?"

Daddy was not convinced. "He's too old for you, Keisha."

"What do you know about him?" Mom asked.

"You've met him—or at least seen him," I tried to explain, trying to be patient. "He works at the school as track and softball coach—remember when you came to pick me up from cross-country practice? That was Jonathan in the parking lot—the tall one."

"Right," said Daddy. "Like I remember a tall dude."

"He was the good-looking one in the designer warm-ups, Mom," I said appealing to her memory.

"I remember him vaguely. He had odd eyes," she mused.

"You let me go skiing with him last week," I was trying to sound reasonable.

"That wasn't a date," Mom countered. "He was the driver for a school trip."

"This isn't a date either!" I tried to explain. "Rhonda and Tyrone are going, and we're going to meet Gerald and Jalani there."

Mom looked at Daddy. "What do you think, Victor?"

He sighed and looked at me. "I don't like it, but I trust Keisha's judgment and good sense." He sounded like he had just told the dentist to pull out all his teeth—with a pair of pliers!

"I don't like it either," Mom added, "and I

don't trust any young man with my daughter. But I do trust her." She looked at me as if she didn't.

I listened and sighed as my parents tried to make a federal case out of a movie with Jonathan Hathaway. I knew that my mother was glad to see that I was at least showing some interest in dating again. She could see I was trying to peek out of the hole I had gone into when Andy died.

"Most of the boys at school are stupid and, believe it or not, Daddy, just interested in 'scoring.'"

Daddy jerked his head around and started to say something, but I don't think he really wanted to go there. Then he sighed, and admitted that I was probably right.

"Jonathan seems to be different, Daddy. He doesn't need to prove anything like the boys in the high school locker room seem to. He talks to me about world affairs and social problems and cultural movements. He's interesting to talk to, and he's interested in me for my ideas. You don't know how pleasant that is. He can quote long passages from the Bible and Shakespeare. The only deep thoughts and current quotations I get from the dudes at school are the words to rap songs."

Mom chuckled, then sighed. "She *is* eighteen now, Victor, and ready to go to college. When do we let her grow up?"

"Not this week," Daddy responded without smiling.

"He's always been a perfect gentleman, Daddy. He has too much to lose not to behave. His father's reputation as well as his own would be on the line."

My father turned to me. "Five years makes a big difference at your age. This guy is a man, and you're still a girl. Men have been known to take advantage of a young girl's foolishness."

"I'm not gonna be foolish, Daddy. What can happen at a movie with a million people there?"

Daddy kissed me on the forehead and smiled. "Just this one time, I'm going to let you go. But I don't want this young man to become a habit. Have fun, Keisha, and come straight home, you hear me?"

"Thanks, Daddy."

Mom still looked doubtful. "What about the next date, and the next one, and the one after that? I don't want this to become a regular thing."

"Mom, I don't even like Jonathan that much—I just want to see the movie. I'm not going to marry him!" I kissed my mother on the cheek and ran upstairs to call Rhonda and Jalani.

Jonathan arrived at seven that evening. Our house was decorated for Christmas, a huge tree in the living room, evergreen garlands roped everywhere, the smell of pine and pleasant surprises in the air. Jonathan was dressed in a soft black cashmere jacket, black silk pants, and obviously expensive leather shoes.

A lemon drop wrapped in licorice, I thought as I let him in the front door. I shook the thought away, trying not to be excited, but his cologne was faint and kinda sexy, and his smile made me shiver in spite of myself.

Jonathan greeted my father, who was unusually quiet, as well as Mom, who also noticed the cologne and the soft clothes and the charming smile. She frowned with worry and general disapproval, but she tried to be understanding. If it wasn't for Andy's death, I knew there was no way that my mom would ever have let me go out with that dude.

I waved good-bye and breathed a sigh of relief as we walked to the Cherokee. The snow from earlier in the month had melted and turned dirty, but new snow was promised for Christmas, which was only four days away.

Rhonda and Tyrone sat cuddled together in the back seat, Gerald and Jalani sat together on the middle seat.

"Hey, I thought you guys were going to meet us there!" I said as I climbed in.

"I offered to drive, since it's still a little

slippery and I've got four-wheel drive," Jonathan explained.

"Cool," I said, as I settled into the front seat with Jonathan. I glanced through his CD box on the seat and checked out his collection—jazz, rock, blues—dozens of sweet sounds. I smiled with quiet satisfaction as we sailed smoothly to the movie theater.

We chattered about school and Christmas and college application deadlines, Jonathan adding just enough to the conversation to fit in, but not enough to act older than we were. Jonathan paid for all of us, even though Gerald and Tyrone pretended to complain, and we entered the darkened movie theater just as the previews finished.

Rhonda whispered to Jalani, "The previews are the best part! I hate it when I miss those."

"Yeah," Jalani agreed. "How am I going to know what I want to see next week? I love the commercialism! I admit it. Sell me something—I'm a pawn of the system!"

I laughed, and the movie came on with a blast of loud music and beautiful scenery. Gerald and Tyrone had wanted to see *Monster Man Six*, but had given in to us girls, who wanted to see the movie that Jonathan had picked out. It was in Italian and had subtitles and was about love and life and miracles. Me and Rhonda and Jalani loved it, of course, and we all cried at the end. Gerald and Tyrone slept through the second half. The first half they kept getting up to get popcorn. Jonathan watched it all, sometimes translating the Italian for me, when the subtitles got to be confusing. Again, I was amazed at him.

"When did you learn Italian?" I asked.

"We lived all over Europe when I was little. I know a little German and French as well," he said modestly. "Dad was career army. He worked his way up through the ranks; he left as a major and an administrator in the army educational system."

"That must have been an exciting child-hood," I said with interest.

"It was awful," Jonathan said bitterly. "My father was never at home. He never could come to my activities at school. He'd travel all over Europe for army events, but there was no time for me."

After the movie, Jonathan talked about it like some kind of movie critic on TV. He argued about the choices the characters had to make, and brought out details that I had never even noticed. I was fascinated, but Tyrone and Gerald looked at Jonathan like they looked at our history teacher—they just hoped he'd shut up soon. They promised they would take Jalani and Rhonda to see *Monster Man Six* during Christmas vacation.

Jonathan dropped off Jalani and Rhonda,

then Tyrone and Gerald. Finally it was just me and Jonathan—alone in the car.

"Did you enjoy it?" he asked me as the music played softly from the back speakers.

"I really did," I admitted. "You know so much, or at least you've got thoughts on so much that it seems like you're really smart."

"Ah," he said smiling, "you have discovered my secret."

I smiled back. "It works," I said quietly. "Don't knock it." I paused, then continued. "Tell me about your mother. How did she like army life?"

Jonathan drove silently through the frosty night. Then he said, with great emotion, "My mother was very lonely, and eventually very bitter about living the army life. She became irritable, short-tempered, and just plain mean. Since my dad wasn't there to yell at most of the time, she took her frustrations out on me. I was never good enough or smart enough or fast enough to please her. I loved her, but it seemed like I couldn't make her love me." He was silent again. "I've said too much," he said finally.

"I'm glad you told me," I said quietly. I was impressed with his honest show of emotion. "Have you and your mom kinda smoothed things out now that you are . . . grown?"

"I haven't seen my mother since I was thirteen, when she and Dad got divorced. She left without saying good-bye." He sighed. "Dad eventually left the military and married a pleasantly plump and sinfully rich woman who spent the rest of my teenage years trying to build up my self-esteem by giving me money to spend and telling me how good-looking I was! So I guess I can't complain."

I smiled and glanced over at Jonathan, who had relaxed a bit. "She's right, you know," I said shyly. I couldn't believe I said that to him!

Jonathan said nothing, but hummed a soft tune as he drove me home. We pulled into my driveway a full half hour before Daddy had told me to be back. My father had strung Christmas lights outside and they looked cheerful and festive against the darkness. I noticed that the light was still on in my parents' bedroom.

"Very pretty," Jonathan said to the darkness.

"Daddy's decorations?" I asked.

"Sure, those, too, but I was talking about you." He looked directly at my face, his golden eyes fastened on my brown ones. I couldn't take it. I dropped my head and blushed. I felt fluttery inside, confused and uncomfortable. I hadn't let myself feel that way since me and Andy had been really happy and tight together, which was months before his death. Jonathan's cologne and the closeness of him in the car was more than I wanted to think about right now.

I grabbed the door handle. "Thanks, Jonathan. I had fun. I really did. I better get inside now before my father comes out here with a grenade," I joked.

He laughed and got out of the car, and walked me carefully to the door. I fumbled for my keys, not sure what was supposed to happen next.

Jonathan smiled at me in the dim glow of the porch light. He had to know how confused and shaky I felt. He touched my cheek gently with his finger, and said simply, "Good night, Keisha." With that, he turned and walked back to his car. I just stood there for a moment, stunned at his gentleness and understanding.

When I walked in the door, Mom was in the kitchen, getting a glass of milk that she probably did not really want. "How was it?" Mom asked, sipping the milk.

"Really nice, Mom," I said with feeling, still musing over the last few moments. "Really nice. We talked about the movie and about when he was a kid. He drove me straight home, and then he touched my cheek and said good night. That's it!"

"That's it?"

"Yeah, not at all like I thought, and certainly not like you and Daddy worried about. He was really cool."

"Sounds wonderful," Mom said without enthusiasm, but she gave me that I-can-see-everything mom look. "Go say good night to your dad. He's been worried, too."

"There's nothing to worry about, Mom," I said with a smile. But as I headed upstairs to speak to my father, a faint frown crossed my face. Jonathan was wonderful—like no one I had ever met—fine and sharp and smart, too. But there was something, something I couldn't put my finger on, that bothered me. I couldn't put it into words, wasn't even sure what I felt. Worry? His childhood? I wasn't sure. But I let the thought pass as I chattered with Daddy about the movie and the uneventful evening.

Jonathan did not call the next day or the next. I wasn't sure if I wanted him to or not, but I found myself thinking about him more than I wanted to admit.

On Christmas Eve, a huge bouquet of red roses, each tied individually with a silver ribbon, was delivered to my house. I squealed with delight, for no one had ever sent me flowers before. *Now that's the difference between a boy and a man!* I thought with pleasure. A real man knew of course how to capture the heart of a lady. I searched for the card, but there was none. I called Rhonda and Jalani, and the three of us tried to decide if I should call Jonathan and thank him. They told me that since he hadn't sent a card, he didn't want to be thanked. Yet. Both girls came over to my house to admire the roses, sniffing them and giggling with me about what they meant. My parents weren't impressed; I think they felt very uncomfortable with this young man who was so clever at pleasing their daughter.

10

On the afternoon of Christmas Eve, I stopped by Monty's house and took him a gift. His mom hugged me and thanked me for always remembering Monty.

"Monty's my man," I replied, laughing. As he got older, he was starting to look more and more like Andy.

"A portable CD player!" Monty cried with joy. "Thanks, Keisha! You're the best!" Monty wanted to be older, to be like the kids in high school. No one could tell him to enjoy being a kid while he could.

I hugged him, remembering Andy as I touched the thick curliness of his hair. "Maybe before Christmas break is over, you can come to the mall with us and pick out a couple of CDs." Monty beamed with pleasure, and hugged me again.

I left Monty's house, thinking of Andy and the past. I drove aimlessly, avoiding the area around Kenwood Mall, where people were jammed shoulder to shoulder grabbing stuff they didn't even like for people they really didn't care about. They had rushed to that last pre-Christmas sale before the after-Christmas sales began. I didn't want to be a part of that mess. I knew that Rhonda was with Tyrone in that crowd, and Angel, along with Joyelle, and Gerald and Jalani were probably there, too.

But I couldn't deal with that today. The malls made Christmas into a hunk of phony plastic wrapped in pretty paper. I wanted to get one last gift for my mother—something real, something not made of plastic. Mom liked flowers. I figured I'd try to find a plant, something that would keep on living long after all the broken Christmas gifts had been returned to the store.

With no particular destination in mind, I drove around, listening to Christmas music on the radio, and thinking about Andy. I ended up downtown, which was surprisingly empty for Christmas Eve. I guess most of the shoppers were in the malls. I stopped in front of a small flower shop with really pretty floral arrangements in the window. *Mom would like this place,* I thought, so I turned off the car and headed inside.

I opened the door to the rich smell of blooms and leaves and soil. Standing behind the desk, snipping the petals of a poinsettia plant, was Leon Hawkins. When he glanced up and saw me, he inhaled in surprise. It's the first time I remember that he didn't even have anything funny to say.

"Hi, Keisha," he said, looking like my cocker spaniel does when I get home from school. "Merry Christmas!"

"Well, hey, Leon. I sure didn't expect to see anyone I knew!" Leon looked surprisingly good standing there—with short, black hair and taut muscles under his snowman T-shirt. I was amazed that I hadn't noticed before. He looked comfortable and relaxed in the flower shop.

"What brings you here?" he asked, smiling shyly.

"I'm not sure, Leon. I was just driving around, thinking about . . . you know, stuff that's happened. I couldn't deal with mall madness today, and I wanted to get my mom a nice plant. And somehow I just found myself here. I had no idea you worked here."

"I know the ghosts of Christmas past can be hard to live with," Leon said gently. "I know all that happened last year is really hard for you to deal with."

"You sound like you've been there," I said quietly. "You're always in such a good mood—laughing and joking around."

"Sometimes I laugh to cover up other stuff," Leon said shyly.

"I'm sorry, Leon," I said, a little embarrassed. "I should know better."

"Hey, don't sweat it!" he said. "I think you're really cool, Keisha, the way you've handled yourself through all this." Leon snipped that poinsettia like a barber working on a man with an afro.

"All I did was survive! There was no great plan. I just live one day at a time." I started to chuckle to myself—the poinsettia had no leaves left.

"Well, you make it look easy. Lots of kids at school admire you."

"Really?" I was genuinely surprised. I decided to change the subject. "How long you been working here?"

"For pay off and on for about six years. I work during summer vacation, weekends, after school, and Christmas break. Before that I'm sure somebody was violating child labor laws 'cause I worked here for no pay at all!" He was smiling again.

"You worked here as a kid without them paying you?" I was confused.

Leon didn't answer at first. "I was just about to close up and go home," he said, still smiling. "The owner left several hours ago." He still seemed nervous and excited that I was there—he snipped the entire top of the poinsettia off and it fell with a soft whoosh to the counter. Both of us burst out laughing.

"I guess you got carried away!" I said. "Don't worry. After tomorrow no one will want a poinsettia anyway!"

"You're right," agreed Leon cheerfully. "Here," he said, shoving two of the red-and-green plants toward me, and a Christmas cactus as well. "Merry Christmas! Take these home to your mom."

"You want to trim them first?" I said, teasing him.

"Yeah, let me go get my chain saw!" he said, laughing. "Seriously, I want your mom to have these."

"Won't your boss mind if you give his plants away?" I asked.

"No," explained Leon. "My boss is my dad. He bought this shop when he got out of college, so I grew up here. I guess it's always been me and my dad. I've hung around this shop all my life. He just started paying me for it when I turned twelve. I love it here—the smells, the beauty, the colors . . . and the way the flowers make people smile." He stopped, looked at me, then turned away.

"I understand, Leon," I replied. I could see how embarrassed he was. "Especially in the winter, blooming flowers bring smiles to folks like me who are sad and confused. Just this morning, I got a huge bouquet of roses delivered to my door and it really made my day!"

"Really?" Leon replied with surprise. "Who were they from?" he asked.

"He didn't sign the card, but I know they were from this guy I went out with one time. They were just beautiful and showed so much class, you know what I mean?"

Leon smiled. "Yeah, I know what you mean. Anything that could make you happy must be dynamite!"

Leon tidied up the shop and turned out the lights. I walked out with him, carrying the plants he had given me, still not sure how I ended up at that particular shop, but glad that I had. As we headed out the door, I asked, "Aren't you going to take a flower for *your* mom, or is she sick of flowers from the shop?"

Leon's smiled faded for a moment, then he shifted back into Leon-the-goofy-joke-teller, a place where it seemed like he felt more comfortable. "I could never play the dozens as a kid, you know," he said instead of answering me. He double-checked the lock of the flower shop door.

"Huh?" I was confused.

"You know, the dozens, where you talk about somebody's mama," he explained.

"Of course I know what the dozens are," I

replied, laughing. "Yo mama wear army boots. Yo mama got bad breath, and so on. But what does that have to do with you?"

Leon tried to act silly, but he just couldn't keep joking. "I could never play the dozens because my mother was honest-to-goodness, straitjacket, rubber-wall crazy. Nuts! Wacko! She would play in the snow in her bare feet and walk to the grocery store butt-naked in a rainstorm! She'd sing real loud and off-key in church during the sermon, and cry during any TV commercial that had a cat in it. She believed she could fly and several times I had to stop her from jumping from windows. All my childhood I tried to cover for her and pretend she was normal, but it's very hard to live with a serious schizophrenic. Finally it got to be more than me and my dad and a whole bus-load of doctors could handle, so she went to live in California at a residential facility that's run by my Aunt Lucy, who's a psychiatrist."

I didn't know what to say. "Is she still there? In California?" I finally asked when Leon said nothing. We were walking slowly out to the street to where I had parked my car.

"No. She loved the ocean, and one day she just decided to become a part of it. Aunt Lucy told us it happened so quickly that no one had time to stop her or save her."

I gasped. "I'm so sorry, Leon. I never knew."

"I've never told anyone else," he said. Then he tried to jump back with a joke. "So now you know why I'm so crazy!" he said, laughing halfheartedly.

"That's not funny!" I told him. "Don't joke like that. It's okay to cry sometimes. Trust me. I do it all the time!"

Leon smiled at me with a look that coulda melted snow. But I kinda understood where he was coming from. He slid on the ice and made himself slip and fall. I laughed and we both felt better—less embarrassed. I helped him up, and he headed down the street, turning to say, "Merry Christmas, Keisha. I guess I'll see you at school after the break."

I was confused. "Where are you parked?"

"Oh, I took the bus this morning. My dad needed the car to finish up the Christmas shopping."

"You think I'm gonna let you wait on the bus in the freezing cold on Christmas Eve? Be for real! Hop in. I'll take you home."

Leon didn't hesitate. "Thanks, Keisha. I was hoping you would, but I didn't want to ask. It was the bus this afternoon, or a skateboard! And it's just too cold to be sliding my behind all over this ice! I know—I tried!"

"Well, what are friends for?" I asked as we got into the car.

"Are we friends, Keisha?" Leon asked quietly.

"Of course we are. I've known you since, since . . ."

"Kindergarten."

"Has it been that long?"

"I've always watched you, Keisha. You were always pretty and popular—like a butterfly—fluttering and shining for others to admire. People like to hang around you. Me, I'm the class fool. I stub my toe in front of the class to get a laugh, or kiss an aardvark at the zoo, or wear my pants and shirt backward to make people laugh."

"I'm glad I've gotten the chance to know you better," I told him. "I'm sorry if I, if I . . . ," I wasn't sure what to say.

"Overlooked me? You didn't. I'm like that tree over there—always hangin' around whether you notice it or not."

"You're pretty poetic," I said with real admiration.

Leon grinned as he directed me to get to his house, which was small and white—and just a couple of miles from mine. He insisted that I come in and meet his dad, who seemed to be delighted to meet me.

"So you're the young lady that Leon seems to be so taken with," his dad began. Leon tried to stop his father from talking, but it was too late.

"You're even prettier than your pictures," Mr. Hawkins added.

I was confused. "Huh?" was all I could say.

"Didn't he tell you? Leon has a bulletin board covered with pictures of you in his room. He's been collecting them for years."

I could see that Leon was about to die of embarrassment. I was amazed at what his dad had spilled, but I knew how parents can sometimes make a bad situation really impossible, so I tried to jump in and help Leon out.

"Leon and I have known each other since kindergarten," I said. "We've always exchanged class pictures. Now that it's our senior year, I'm glad to finally meet you."

Leon glanced at me with a look that said, *Thanks big-time for not flipping out about this.*

I smiled back with a look that said, *No sweat—I got you covered.* After refusing his dad's offer to help decorate their tree, I told them I had to get home to help my mother finish wrapping gifts, which was at least partially true.

"I hope you don't think I'm some kind of weirdo, Keisha," he said to me at the door. "I've always admired you. That's all."

"It's nice to know, Leon. Actually, I think it's kinda cool. I'm just not sure how to act."

"Just be yourself. I'll continue to be the kid that goes out for the giggles, and you continue to be the butterfly in the bloom. I'll be there for you if you ever need me. Know that."

"I believe you, Leon." I smiled at him with newfound admiration. "Merry Christmas, and thanks for a really unexpected Christmas gift. There is nothing more important than a friend." I kissed him lightly on the cheek and left.

I thought about Leon all the way home—what a genuinely nice guy he was, how rough his childhood must have been, and how special it made me feel that he seemed to think so much of me. *Strange,* I thought. *Very strange.* When I called Jalani and Rhonda that evening, I only told them that I had run into Leon and given him a ride home. I wasn't sure why, but I left out the rest of the story. Some things, I decided, are meant to be kept secret.

11

Christmas morning dawned cold and snowy. Several inches had fallen overnight, and my yard looked like one of those pictures on a Christmas card as I peeked out of the window. My parents were still asleep and wouldn't be up for hours. When I was little, I used to get them up right at sunrise, but as I got older, I started letting them sleep while I got up and fixed breakfast. Gifts could wait. I kinda liked sitting alone in the morning quiet, watching the snow.

The phone rang, startling me. "Merry Christmas!" I said cheerfully as I picked it up.

"Keisha? This is Mrs. Washington, Joyelle's mom. Have you seen her or talked to her recently?" Her voice was tight and shaking. "I've called Angel and a couple of her other friends, but no one knows anything."

"No, I haven't," I replied with concern. "I haven't talked to her since we got out of school for Christmas break. What's wrong?"

"One car is gone, and so is Joyelle." Mrs. Washington burst into tears. "I can't take this. If something has happened to her, I will just die. I can't take this!" she wailed.

I knew that Joyelle couldn't drive. She hadn't had lessons and wasn't old enough to have a driver's license. This was not good.

I couldn't believe that I was trying to calm an adult down, but I tried to calm down Joyelle's mom as best I could. "I'm sure she's okay, Mrs. Washington. Have you called the police?"

"Yes, of course, and my husband is out looking for her. Please call all your friends and find out if any of them has seen her. And please call me back if you hear anything. Anything at all."

"I will, Mrs. Washington," I promised.

Just then, she said, "Wait, the other line is beeping. Hold on. This might be my husband from his cell phone." The line was silent for a moment.

Mrs. Washington returned to the line, hardly able to speak for the huge sobbing gulps. "Joyelle has been in an accident. She was driving her father's car and has been taken to Good Samaritan Hospital. I'm on my way there now." She hung up.

I felt like a rock hit my gut—memories of another phone call that I had tried to forget rushed to me and my heart began to beat way too fast.

I called Angel and Gerald's house. Gerald answered the phone. "Gerald, they found Joyelle." I paused and took a deep breath. "She's been in an accident in her dad's car. She's at Good Samaritan."

"Oh, no!" Gerald groaned. "Angel is gonna be really wiped out about this. You goin' down there?"

"Yeah, I'm on my way. I'll see you there." I hung up the phone, woke my parents to tell them what had happened, and headed downtown to the hospital. The beauty of the snow now seemed just harsh and cold. I tried not to think, tried not to cry.

By the time I got to the emergency room, Mrs. Washington was sitting in a chair, crying softly. All she could do was mumble the names "Robbie" and "Joyelle" over and over again. Mr. Washington sat on the other side of the room, biting his fingernails.

Gerald and Angel got there right after I did. Angel looked scared. Gerald walked over to Mr. Washington and took his hand. He said nothing. I remember when Gerald and Angel had to go to court about their stepfather, Mr.

Washington had been there for them. The older man returned Gerald's firm grip and thanked him silently.

The doctor emerged then, called the Washingtons to a small room, and talked to them in whispers. Then he escorted them to the back area where Joyelle had been taken. They were only gone for a few minutes, but it seemed like forever.

Mr. and Mrs. Washington returned finally, not holding hands, but both smiling through their tears. "She's going to be fine," Mr. Washington said to us. His voice held a relief that was so great it could be squeezed. "She was saved by the air bag and the seat belt. She has only minor cuts and bruises."

Our sigh of relief could have filled a huge balloon.

"Is she conscious?" Angel asked fearfully, remembering her own bout with the hospital just a few weeks before.

"Oh yes," Mrs. Washington assured her. "She's wide awake, crying profusely, and terrified that she's in more trouble than she's ever been in her life. Which she is." She laughed a little then, mostly in relief. "I'm so glad that she's not hurt that I don't know if I can punish her."

"Can we see her?" Angel asked. Mr. Washington glanced at the doctor who was standing nearby.

"I don't see why not," the doctor said, "but just for a few minutes. We're going to run a couple of tests before we let her go home." He directed us to an area behind a blue-striped curtain. Joyelle lay there, looking pale and scared. Two Band-Aids decorated her forehead, and an IV ran into her arm.

"Hey, Joyelle," Angel said shyly. "You tryin' to take the attention from me?"

"No, girl," Joyelle replied. "I just wanted to see what tearing up my Daddy's brand-new Lincoln Continental on Christmas Day would be like!" She smiled a little.

"What happened?" I asked. Joyelle glanced at her parents, who nodded for her to continue. She sighed. "Christmas was gonna be horrible anyway. Mom and Dad were fighting all the time, and I missed Rob so much I wanted to scream. It seemed like nobody cared. I found Dad's keys on the kitchen counter, and at first, I just wanted to sit in his car and listen to music. Then I got cold, so I put the keys into the ignition and turned the motor on. I just sat there, imagining myself driving on the open road in Canada or someplace like that."

Joyelle continued, "It was so easy to put my foot on the brake and move the gear shift to reverse. The car rolled into the empty street like it knew what to do. I wasn't even thinking. I was mad at Rob for being dead and mad at both of you, Mommy and Daddy, for everything at home being so messed up. I put on my seat belt, drove to the corner, and stopped at the stop sign. Then I just kept going. It was a piece of cake! I didn't know where I was and I didn't care. I just wanted to keep driving forever." Her mother was crying again.

"I guess I drove about five miles. I saw this car coming, and I figured it would stop, so I turned left, but I guess it didn't stop. I heard a horn, and a crunching sound, and that's all I remember."

The room was silent. Angel and I looked at each other. Gerald quietly headed back to the waiting room. Mr. Washington looked at his wife then, and reached to take her hand. "Barbara, I hope that nothing will break up this family ever again. We have to learn to cherish what we have. I love Joyelle, and I love you." Then he kissed her tenderly on the lips, right in front of us. Angel and I tiptoed out of that room then—this was a family matter.

I thought that was the most beautiful scene I had ever witnessed. True love, in spite of difficulties. *That's the way a relationship ought to be,* I thought. *The way me and Andy might have been.*

We all went back home then, some of us to open gifts, some to give thanks that Christmas still had something to celebrate. I hadn't opened any of my gifts when the phone call came, so I pulled up into my driveway with real joy and expectation. I had called my parents and told them that Joyelle was going to be fine, but that her dad's car was in pretty bad shape. "Cars can be fixed," Mom said wisely. "People can't." I knew that all too well.

As I walked to the front door, I noticed a small red package tied with silver ribbon sitting on the door mat. I picked it up, saw that my name was engraved on the card, but again, no other name. I took it inside and ran upstairs to my room. I didn't immediately show it to my mother, although I did stop to give both parents a big hug and tell them I loved them. "Life is too short to forget that," I told them as I breezed out of their room. Parents like that kind of stuff.

I sat on my bed and slowly unwrapped the package. The silver ribbon was similar to the ribbon that had decorated the roses. The red wrapping paper was thick and expensive, with decorations so deeply embossed that I could trace the design with my fingers. I unfolded it carefully to find a red velvet box hidden beneath the layers of paper. I gasped at the beauty of the box. I was afraid to imagine what was inside. I opened the lid of the small box slowly. Inside was a tiny silver butterfly, delicate and shimmering on a thin silver chain. I smiled with delight. *That Jonathan was something special,* I thought. I put the box away, in the back of my underwear drawer. I didn't show my mother, who probably wouldn't approve and definitely wouldn't understand.

12

In January the temperature stayed below zero for two weeks. I hardly felt the cold, however. I spent my evenings filling out college applications after I finished my homework, then I waited, with increasing anticipation, for Jonathan to call. The calls had started slowly, right after Christmas, but it wasn't long before he was calling every night. He was so interesting to talk to—with tales of other countries, strange cultures, music, language, even philosophy.

I never thanked him for the flowers or the butterfly necklace, but he never mentioned them, so I just never brought the subject up. I figured he had his reasons for wanting to keep them a secret, maybe because he knew my parents might not approve, or maybe because he liked the idea of secret surprises.

He hadn't asked me out since the triple movie date, but that was fine with me, and certainly fine with my parents, who had no idea that I was talking to Jonathan every single night. They knew I was on the phone, but it never occurred to them that I was spending hours after dark talking to Jonathan Hathaway.

One night he called me and said, in that bass voice that made me shiver with delight, "How do you know you exist, Keisha?"

"'Cause I'm lookin' at myself, and I can see I'm sitting here," I told him.

"Suppose you couldn't see. Would you still be there?"

I was quiet for a minute. This was one of those philosophical brain busters that Jonathan liked to create. "Of course," I said. "I could still feel my body with my hands, so I'd still be there even if I couldn't see myself." I could almost feel him grinning on the other end of the line.

"Suppose you couldn't feel yourself at all—say you're wrapped in a cocoon and can't move. Do you still exist?"

This was fun. It made me think, made me use all my brain cells. "Well, I guess other people could see me. They would know I existed, right?"

"Okay. Suppose," Jonathan continued, "all of them swore you weren't there, ignored you. Do you still exist?"

"This is crazy! Yes, I exist," I insisted. "I can see stuff, smell the air, hear the sounds of the people who are ignoring me. So that proves it."

Jonathan paused for effect. "Suppose," he went on, drawing me deeper, "all of your senses are taken away. You can't see or hear, can't smell, taste, or touch."

"Not much of an existence," I said. "I guess the only thing that can't be taken away is my mind, my ability to think. So as long as I can think, I exist!"

"Congratulations!" Jonathan told me with pride. "You just got an *A* in advanced philosophy. That was our exam question last semester."

"And I got it right?" I was amazed.

"Of course. You're brilliant, Keisha. I've never met anyone quite like you."

I was grinning into the phone like he could see me. Jonathan made me feel like a grown-up with a mind, not a girl with a phone number like the boys I'd meet at the mall did. At school, I often saw Jonathan in the halls. He was always dressed like a model out of *GQ*, and he always bowed when he saw me.

Rhonda and Jalani giggled whenever he did that and thought it was really cool. "That dude sure can rag tough! He can go shopping with me anytime." Rhonda said, teasing me. I was a little embarrassed, but pleased.

I even started dressing differently when we went to school after Christmas break. Instead of jeans and T-shirts, I started wearing tailored slacks and silk blouses. It made me feel kinda mature, like I was ready to be responsible or something. I figured it was about time to leave the high school girl behind. I had no idea what a college girl was supposed to look like, or act like, but I was gonna figure it out. Rhonda told me that I was trying to dress like Jonathan, but I told her, "I dress to please myself."

One day I ran into Leon Hawkins in the hall. We didn't have any classes together this year, but I saw him at lunch and sometimes after school. I gave him a big hug. He spun around in the hall like an ice skater does in his routine, bounced himself off a row of lockers with a huge rattling commotion, and grinned.

"How's it goin', Leon?" I asked as he picked himself up from the floor.

"Things are cookin'!" he cheerfully replied. "I just got admitted to Morehouse— early decision! I'm charged!"

"Hey! That's awesome! I'm so proud of you! I just mailed my application to Spelman, so I guess it will be awhile before I know if I'll be joining you in Atlanta. I applied to four other colleges, too."

"Where?" asked Leon.

"Oh, the University of Cincinnati, of course, Miami, Georgetown, and Pepperdine in California."

"Wow, those are some good schools. Hey, you look dynamite, Keisha—different somehow," Leon told me.

I blushed and grinned. "I guess I'm just learning to be happy again. It's a good feeling." I was in kind of a hurry, so I rushed on down the hall.

"Take care," he called after me.

That evening, I got a call from Joyelle. Everybody at school, of course, had heard about her Christmas Day accident. I think some of the ninth graders even admired her for driving a Lincoln Continental for several miles without hitting anything. The older kids were amazed that she had lived to tell about it.

"How you feelin', Joyelle?" I asked her as I looked in the refrigerator for a snack.

"Much better today. I'm more embarrassed than anything," she admitted. "I was really stupid."

"You got that right," I told her. "You can't be doin' stuff like that to your folks. Parents can't handle too much, you know."

"Yeah, I know. Hey, Keisha, let me ask you something. I was talking to Leon Hawkins in the hall today. And he says to me, 'I know all the girls in this school got some kind of invisible hotline that links you all with pagers and phones and voice mail and stuff. Probably E-mail, too.'" I laughed, 'cause he had it just about right.

"Yep!" I said.

"Then he says, 'And I know that all of you somehow know every single relationship in the building. You know who's talkin' to who, who's got no chance, and who's got possibilities.'"

"Leon said all this to you?" I asked, a little surprised.

"Let me finish, Keisha! I say to him, 'I know where you're going—this is about Keisha, right?'"

"You're kidding!" I said.

"If I'm lyin', I'm flyin'!" Joyelle said. "Then he says to me, 'I feel stupid having to ask a ninth grader, but I know you got the connections and information.'"

"So what did you say then?"

"I told him, 'If you're trying to talk to Keisha, give it up. She's hooked up to something that's not even in your league, not even in a high school league anymore. You know what I'm saying?'"

"What did he say?" This was pretty amazing.

"He just frowned and said, 'It just ain't

141

cool for a coach to be hitting on a student, even if he is the principal's son. Big phony—all that bowin' and grinnin'—makes me want to puke.' Then he went on to class." Joyelle really sounded like she was glad to be able to tell me all this. I knew that as soon as she hung up, she'd be on the phone to every girl she knew—telling them the story.

"He had to know that you would tell me. It sounds like he wanted me to know."

"You didn't know he liked you?" Joyelle asked.

"Yeah, I did, sorta. He's nice, even kinda cute, but he's just a kid—you know what I mean?" Just then my line beeped to let me know that I had another call. I clicked over, found it was Jonathan, and told Joyelle I had to go.

"Hi, Jonathan," I said. I'm glad he couldn't see me grinning like a stupid kid.

"Hello, my butterfly," Jonathan said, his voice as smooth as silk. "How are you keeping warm on this bright and chilly day?"

I tried not to sound childish and excited, but he didn't know how close he came to truth when he called me that; his voice made my stomach feel like it was full of butterflies. "I'm dressed in dirty sweats, sipping hot tea, and dreaming of the Bahamas!" I answered, laughing.

"Slip into some clean sweats and let me

take you to the museum. There's a special display of Romantic and Impressionist art, and I want you to see it."

"Right now? My parents aren't even home from work yet," I told him, but I immediately ripped off my dirty sweats and opened my closet for a fresh pair of jeans.

"We'll be back in two hours—I promise," he said in a tone that seemed to indicate he knew that I was already digging frantically for my purple sweater. "Leave your parents a note. Just tell them that you had to go to the museum for a homework assignment, which is not completely untrue. I'll be by in ten minutes."

"I'll be ready," I heard myself say.

"See you." Almost before the phone had dropped back into the receiver, I rushed into the bathroom to brush my teeth, pin up my hair, and douse a slight spray of Earthen Essence cologne behind each ear. *But of course, I'm not excited,* I kept telling myself.

I left a garbled note for my parents which talked vaguely about a school project, grabbed the new leather jacket that I got for Christmas, and closed the front door just as Jonathan pulled into the drive. He grinned, jumped out to open the door on my side, and I eased into the warmth and soft leather smell of his Cherokee.

"You look wonderful," Jonathan murmured as he leaned over to help me with my seat belt. I didn't need the help, but I let him anyway. He paused to look directly into my eyes. It seemed like he was going to just dissolve me with those golden hazel eyes. I was the first to look away. I was finding it hard to breathe.

He moved back into place in the driver's seat, and drove smoothly and silently to the museum. He hummed along with the music on the CD and turned to smile at me at every red light. I put my hand to my face while he wasn't looking, feeling my face for zits or blackheads. I wondered if toothpaste was as effective as mouthwash, if early-morning deodorant really lasted all day, and if my hairstyle looked like some kind of junior high school kid's.

The art exhibit, as he promised, was awesome. He guided me through the pieces, telling interesting stories about the artists, pointing out colors where I hadn't noticed them and details that I had overlooked by simply blinking. I was amazed and impressed and stimulated—so many colors and sights swirling in my brain, the pale cool tones of the artwork, the touch of his hand on mine, the scent of his cologne, the soft silkiness of his shirt, the warmth of his breath on my ear as he whispered another secret about an artist. I felt melted, soft, and alive.

As we left the museum, the cold crisp air

jolted me back to reality somewhat, but I still felt peacefully mellow. Jonathan glanced over at me, seemed to know exactly how I felt, so he asked me softly, "Would you like to get a cup of coffee?"

I said yes before I thought about the fact that my parents had been home for more than an hour and that I never drank coffee. We drove to the university district to a coffee house that had tables hand-painted by local college students, a menu written on a chalkboard, and the deep rich smell of espresso permanently absorbed into the wooden walls. The music was loud reggae, and the crowd was subdued and sophisticated. He ordered two espressos and I drank that rich powerful stuff like I'd done it all my life. It warmed me all the way down to my socks.

"That espresso might keep you up tonight," he warned. "It's pretty strong."

"I don't mind," I said. "I have so much to think about—I don't know if I'll ever sleep again."

"Your mind is so open and ready to absorb everything, Keisha," he said with admiration. "You're like a plant that has been parched and dry, waiting for the rain to help you bloom."

"Are you my rain?" I asked him teasingly.

"I'm a full-blast thunderstorm," he replied, teasing back. "Can you handle it?"

The conversation seemed to have double meaning, but I wasn't exactly sure where it was headed. "I'm not sure," I answered him honestly. "But I'm having a dynamite time finding out."

Jonathan reached over and touched my hand. His touch was almost as electric as a lightning bolt. "You are like no one I have ever met, Keisha."

The waitress, a girl with a pierced nose, eyebrow, and lip, interrupted. "You two lovebirds want anything else?"

I blushed and snatched my hand away. Jonathan just paid the bill and touched me on the elbow to guide me out of the crowded place. On the way home, I was quiet, but my heart was pounding, partly from the coffee, and partly from the stimulation of Jonathan's hand on my knee as he drove. I didn't try to remove it, even though I knew I probably should. Somehow, it just felt right.

He drove, smiling at me occasionally. "I want to show you something," he murmured. He drove up a steep hill through Eden Park and parked the wagon on the edge of an overlook. The view was breathtaking. The entire city was spread out beneath us, decorated in snow and lights. I had seen the view before, but not with my heart pounding to the pulsing beats coming from Jonathan's CD player. Then he leaned over me like he did when I first got in the car, as if to help me with my seat belt, but this time when he paused to look into my eyes, I didn't look away.

The look became a breath, then a sigh, then a kiss. I felt a heat that chilled me, and a strength that left me weak, as I melted into the cushion of the seat of his car. My blood felt like it was turning to oil. I was melting, I knew. But he just smothered all my thoughts as I answered his kiss, hesitantly at first, but soon I was whirled into the power of his arms. Suddenly I got frightened, and I pulled away from him, which made me feel foolish and immature.

"What's wrong?" he whispered.

"It's getting late," I managed to stammer. "I better get home. I'm sorry."

"No problem," Jonathan replied quickly. He backed the car away from the overlook and headed out of the park. He clicked the CD player off with a sharp twist of his hand and we rode the rest of the way to my house in silence.

I wasn't sure if he was mad at me, at himself, or if he even cared. I wasn't sure if I had done the right thing. Would he lose interest in me now? And I wasn't sure how I felt. His kiss and embrace had been the most exciting, most powerful experience I've ever known, but it made me a little uncomfortable. *Quit acting like a kid*, I told myself. *You're eighteen years old. Grow up!* But I didn't feel very grown-up. I felt confused, scared, and very, very young.

When we got to my driveway, I could see my mother peeping through the curtains. I could tell she was really pissed. "I better run. Mom's got fire coming out of her eyes. I had a *wonderful* time, Jonathan! And I'm sorry if I . . ." I didn't know what to say.

He managed to smile. I couldn't tell if he was upset or just being polite. "I'll call you after midnight," he promised. "On your cell phone." I breathed a sigh of relief. *Maybe I haven't screwed up,* I told myself with relief. I hurried up the snowy steps to face my mother's anger.

13

"**Where have you been,** young lady?" my mother demanded.

"At the art museum. Honest! What's the big deal?" I'd never spoken to Mom like that before. Either the coffee or the kiss had made me bolder than usual.

"Don't you speak to me in that tone of voice," Mom warned. "Why didn't you call me?"

"I left you a note." I was angry.

"I've been home for three hours!" my mother continued. "The art museum closed at five. Did you go to the library?"

I started to lie, but decided not to, even though I knew the truth would get me in trouble. I felt rebellious, and my uneasiness about Jonathan made me turn my fears into words that I shot like bullets at my mother. "I went to a coffee shop by the university. And then I stopped by Eden Park."

"A coffee shop? That's not your usual hangout." I could tell Mom didn't like the tone of voice that I was using. "Who did you go with? Rhonda?"

"No." I was silent for a moment. "I went with Jonathan Hathaway," I said finally. It made me feel good to see the anger and disapproval on Mom's face.

Now it was her turn to be silent. "Explain," she finally said. Her voice was sharp like a razor. She was really angry.

I looked at my mother, but didn't answer right away. I took off my coat and hung it up in the closet. While my back was turned, I wiped my lips with my gloves—just to make sure I didn't have any smeared lipstick to make this situation worse. "Jonathan called me and told me about the Impressionist exhibit at the art museum and asked me if I wanted to go," I began. "You weren't home to ask, and I wanted to go," I added sharply. "The exhibit was really good—he knows so much about art," I continued. I was starting to get excited in spite of my anger at my mother. "Then we went to a coffee shop. I had one cup of coffee. We stopped by the park to talk for a few minutes. Then he brought me home. That's all we did. No big deal."

"But what *is* a big deal," Mom responded, "is that you didn't call me and let me know where you were and who you were with. That's all I've ever asked you to do. And you know how I feel about that young man. He's too old for you and too . . . smooth. He worries me."

"He is *not* too old!" I argued. "I am eighteen years old! I'm grown and I can see who I like! I can take care of myself! When are you going to let me grow up?"

"You think you're grown-up, Keisha," my mother sighed, "but if you have to tell people you're an adult, that means you're not. Grown folks never say, 'I'm grown.'"

I refused to accept anything she said, but I was tired of fighting. "I'm sorry, Mom," I said. "Time just disappeared. Jonathan is different. He's smart and I like talking to him. And he makes me feel special."

"How often do you talk to him, Keisha?" Mom asked. It seemed like she was also losing steam with the argument.

"Maybe once a week," I lied. I couldn't let Mom know about the phone calls. She would make them stop and I didn't think I could bear not to be able to talk to Jonathan every day. I refused to think yet about whether he would call tonight after what had happened earlier.

Mom eyed me suspiciously, but decided to drop it for the moment. "I pay good money for that cell phone. You use it to let me know where you are, you hear me?"

"I will," I said. *Tonight after midnight!* I said to myself.

"And keep it turned on. I tried to call you, but it was turned off. That's annoying and could be dangerous."

"I will, Mom. Can I go to my room now? I have to go to the bathroom." I headed up the steps to my room, but I turned to her to say, "I'm sorry, Mom. I just got carried away."

No matter how mad she got at me, Mom always melted when I apologized or told her I loved her. I could see the fire burning out. "Be careful, Keisha," Mom warned. "Don't let this go too far. He's so much older than you are. That frightens me."

Excites me, I thought.

"Don't let this Jonathan fellow overwhelm you."

Too late, I thought. *I think he's got my heart.* I ran up the stairs to wait for midnight and his call.

Later, lying in bed, nestled under my thick blankets and bedspreads, I was wide awake. The coffee had made me feel alive and aware of every sound—the bare branch that scraped my bedroom window, the water dripping from the sink in the bathroom down the hall, the faint creaking of the house as it settled into a long, cold night.

The phone rang and Jonathan's voice, as

usual, melted my guts. "Let me paint you a picture," he began. He didn't mention the incident from earlier in the evening as I was afraid he would. But he never began a conversation like other people who just said what was on their mind. He always spoke to me in stories or ideas. I loved it.

"What colors are you using?" I asked, playing along.

"Pink, mauve, tender peach, and strawberry," he answered. I could hear him smack his lips as he spoke.

"Sounds like it tastes good, too."

"*You* are what tastes good, Keisha."

My heart began to pound again. I was afraid to speak. "I thought you were angry with me," I stammered. I felt stupid and childish.

"Why should I be angry with a beautiful woman? A woman of color and passion?" Jonathan replied smoothly.

I was so relieved and pleased that tears came to my eyes. "Can I ask you something, Jonathan?"

"Anything."

"When you look at me, do you see a woman or a high school girl?" I was sorry I asked as soon as the words left my mouth.

Jonathan's voice filled the darkness as I snuggled under the covers. "I see you as no one else can. I see a woman on the edge of her

153

tomorrow—a woman of beauty and power."

"Are you sure you're looking at me?" I giggled in spite of my attempts to sound mature.

"The boys at school look at you as if you were one of them. You need someone who can see you for the woman that you are."

"And that's you?" I asked.

"If you will let me be the one," he answered humbly.

Again, I didn't know what to say. "You never finished describing your painting," I whispered, trying to make the conversation a little easier to handle.

I could tell he sensed that as he smoothly murmured, "The painting is of you and me. There is light in the distance, and a scented candle very close to us—the smell of lavender. The rest is colors—rainbow colors."

I closed my eyes. I could almost smell the scent of the candle. "And what are we doing?" I asked hesitantly.

"We are holding hands. Kissing. Touching. We are inhaling the scent of the lavender and of ourselves."

I was terrified of how direct he was, but I was excited at the same time. It was so easy to play these delicious games with Jonathan as I lay snuggled safely in my own bedroom. "Perhaps one day," I whispered into the darkness, "you can really paint that picture." I was amazed at my boldness and glad he couldn't see the embarrassed blush on my face.

"Oh, I will," he promised, "and you'll learn the difference between a high school boy and a man who knows how to please a woman."

I turned on my bedroom light. This was getting too heavy for me. "Don't talk like that," I said. "You make me nervous."

"There's nothing to be afraid of," his smooth voice soothed. "Remember, you're not like the rest of the girls. They're still crawling around like caterpillars. You are already a butterfly—ready to try her wings."

Relaxing a bit, I giggled quietly, so as not to wake my parents. I started to mention the silver butterfly necklace that Jonathan had left for me, but now I felt ashamed that I had never thanked him for it. I decided to wear it the next time we went out. "The Valentine Dance is next month," I said instead, changing the subject.

"I know. I have to chaperone. But I promise one dance with you."

"I wasn't going to go," I told him. I didn't really find any fun at school dances anymore. Not since Andy died.

"Oh, no. Please go," Jonathan begged. "I couldn't bear having to watch all those giggling teenagers without you to look at across the room and imagine us, dancing all alone on that dance floor, the music playing just for us."

"What a nice thought!" I answered,

pleased with the compliment. "I guess I will go then." I was starting to get sleepy, and the battery on my phone was getting low.

"Keisha?" His voice never ceased to fascinate me.

"Yes, Jonathan?"

"After the dance, do you have to go straight home?"

"No, we usually go and get something to eat at Waffle House. Sometimes we go bowling. Depends on our mood, but my parents are pretty relaxed about curfews on those nights. At least they used to be."

"Was your mother really mad about you coming in late tonight?"

"Yeah, we went at it. It's hard for her to realize I'm eighteen and leaving for college in a few months. She still wants to treat me like a baby." My anger and sense of injustice had started to return.

"It's hard to raise parents these days. Lord knows I've had trouble enough with my own." Jonathan chuckled. "Make your life easier. Give in to what she wants."

"You're right," I agreed. "But she still made me mad—challenging me like that."

"You're her daughter—she has that right. And she loves you." He changed the subject. "So, after the dance, since I can't officially escort you, why don't you let me take you out to eat? I promise to get you home in plenty of time."

"I'd like that, Jonathan."

"We can't really leave from school," he reasoned, "so how about if I pick you up from your house right after the dance? I hate sneaking like this."

I sighed. "Me, too. But I do want to be able to spend more time with you. Talking to you is always . . . let me find the right word . . . so stimulating!" I knew he was grinning on the other end of the line. "Where will we go to eat?" I asked.

"Someplace 'stimulating,'" he teased. "I've got something just a little more sophisticated than Waffle House in mind," he said mysteriously. "You'll love it, I promise."

"I'm looking forward to it, Jonathan," I said softly. "You make me feel alive again. I've needed that."

"My pleasure," he replied. "Truly my pleasure. Good night, Keisha."

"Good night, Jonathan." I fell asleep dreaming of paintings come alive with color and sound.

14

The next evening after school, I sat in Rhonda's kitchen with Tyrone, Jalani, and Rhonda doing homework. We were in the same English class and the teacher wanted everybody to do a poetry project. Group projects are time wasters, as far I can tell, but teachers seem to like them because it takes so long to give the reports in class. We like them because they're a real low-stress kind of assignment.

Tyrone thought poetry was stupid. Rhonda believed just the opposite. "I like poetry, Tyrone," she told him as they searched for poems to put in our project book. "It makes the world look pretty."

"You're supposed to like it," he countered. "You're a girl."

"What's that supposed to mean? Most of the poets, if you notice, are men!" I said.

"Why would a grown man want to write poetry?" Tyrone asked.

"Because maybe he was in love and he had no other way to tell the woman!" Rhonda answered in exasperation.

"He could have called her on the phone," Tyrone said, spinning the book on his fingers like he spun his basketball. "It's better with a basketball," he mumbled to himself as the book went crashing to the floor. We cracked up.

"Most of these poems were written before they had telephones, stupid," Jalani said as she typed stuff on her laptop.

"So how were you supposed to call up your girl?" he asked, teasing her.

"You stopped by her home, with flowers, after you had received permission from her father," I explained, picking up the poetry book.

"Bummer. Too much trouble. You got anything to drink in your fridge?" he asked Rhonda. He got up and looked in the refrigerator for a soda.

"Wouldn't you have done that for me?" Rhonda asked, teasing him. She grabbed the soda and shook it vigorously.

"You're gonna make purple pop stains on your mama's ceiling!" he warned as he grabbed the soda from her. "And yeah, I woulda done all that for you—and more!

You're worth it, baby. I would have crawled on my hands and knees and licked the floor in order to get permission to see you."

"Now that's romantic!" Jalani said. She and I smiled as Rhonda leaned over to kiss Tyrone on the cheek.

"How'd I get stuck in a group with a bunch of poetry-loving girls?" he moaned.

"You just one lucky dude," I told him.

"You're lucky you got me!" Rhonda teased.

He grabbed Rhonda and tried to kiss her, but she pulled away laughing and threatened to open the shaken can of soda in his face. "Let's get back to work," she reminded him.

He flopped back into a kitchen chair and sighed. "Seriously," he complained, "math makes sense. Lines are straight. They form nice neat angles. They make squares or triangles. I like that. I can understand that. Poetry is full of squiggles and blips. Don't make sense to me."

"Most relationships don't go in a straight line," I tried to explain to him. "Poetry is about feelings, and relationships, and that's really complicated."

"But poetry is so hard! Why can't they just say what they mean instead of all that symbolism and crap?"

"Actually, poetry is easier. It uses fewer words," Jalani added.

"Huh? You're not makin' any sense."

We were all trying to make him understand. Rhonda couldn't do math like Tyrone could, so she understood his frustration. It was how she felt in math every day. So she tried to make him see. "Look at this newspaper article about these girls in Yugoslavia who got raped. It's long and full of words," Rhonda explained slowly.

"So? I understand that. That was a terrible thing that happened to them."

"Stay with me here," Rhonda continued, as she flipped through the poetry book. "Now read this poem here. 'The mothers silently mourn with their weeping daughters.' Eight words. Pure feeling. Do you get it?" she asked him hopefully.

"Yeah, makes me feel uncomfortable," Tyrone said, shifting in his chair. "I hate thinkin' about stuff like that." He paced around the kitchen.

"So it works, right?" Jalani asked.

Tyrone refused to give in. "But what if I'd rather have information instead of feeling? I never seen no sports page done in poetry."

"And you probably never will," I said, trying to help. "But look at this picture of Michael Jordan making this shot. He's three feet off the ground and the ball never touches the net. That's beautiful. That's poetry."

"There's no words," Tyrone reminded me triumphantly.

"Not necessary. The feeling is there. That's what poetry is."

"So let's just cut out pictures and get this project over with!" Tyrone suggested, tossing the book on the floor once more.

"No," Rhonda insisted. "We gotta find words that are as clear as that picture—words that take away everything but the feeling and the beauty."

"Then we ought to just put in a picture of you!" he said as he grabbed her and pulled her into the living room.

"Now that kiss was poetry!" we heard her say after a long silence. Me and Jalani sat quietly in the kitchen and giggled. They didn't seem to care that we were sitting in the next room. "You are so fine, Rhonda. Now this is poetry I can deal with!" we heard him say.

Just then Rhonda heard her mother coming down the stairs, so she pulled away from Tyrone, and they rushed back into the kitchen. Tyrone bent his head in deep concentration in his book, while Rhonda looked at Jalani's laptop and pretended to check a file. Her mother, who was no fool, took one look at us and declared, "Tyrone, you'd get a lot more out of that book if it weren't upside-down."

He looked up and sheepishly turned the book around. "I was going to show it to Rhonda, and I guess I sorta fell asleep."

Rhonda started to laugh, but the look on

her mother's face cut the laughter short. "I know that you two care about each other," her mother said bluntly. "And I know how good it feels when you're young and you want each other like fire." Rhonda had to bow her head and blush. Her mother had never been one to play around with words.

"But I want the two of you to consider the consequences. Sex is serious. And sex can be stupid. Be careful. That goes for you and Jalani, too, Keisha. You kids better think with your heads, not your other body parts." With a final look at Rhonda that let her know she'd hear a lot more later on, her mother left the room. But she left the kitchen door open. We sat there in openmouthed amazement for a minute or two.

"Your mama don't play!" Jalani said.

"You got that right," I added.

"She's right, you know," Rhonda said quietly.

"I know," Tyrone agreed, sighing. "It's rough sometimes, though." He shifted in the kitchen chair, scraping it hard on the floor.

"We've all been there, Tyrone," I said, not sure how much he wanted to discuss.

"Not many dudes are as cool as you, Tyrone," Rhonda said.

He smiled at her as if she were made of sweet caramel. "I ain't embarrassed to tell your friends how I feel about you. You all tell

163

each other everything on the phone anyway!" We laughed. He was right.

He said to Rhonda, "I liked you before I loved you, and I respected you before I needed you. I want to be proud of *my* lady when she walks down the aisle in that white dress. I want it to mean something real!"

"That was poetry what you just said," Rhonda told him, blushing.

"It was?"

"That was pure emotion, Tyrone," I said. "That's poetry!"

"Hey, this poetry stuff is pretty deep. It's not so bad!"

"You are one in a million, Tyrone. I love you." Rhonda was dancing around the kitchen like a firefly.

He whispered across the kitchen table, "You're worth waiting for." The phone rang then, shattering the mood. It was Gerald. Rhonda put him on the speaker phone.

"What's up with the poetry posse?" Gerald asked cheerfully.

"Just chillin'," Rhonda told him. "Studying with Tyrone here in the kitchen."

"Yeah, right. I know how much studying you two be doing."

"Hey, me and Keisha are here, too," Jalani said. "We're keeping them in line." Gerald laughed.

"Besides, my mother comes in to get

something out of the refrigerator every fifteen minutes," Rhonda added.

"Is everybody going to the Valentine Dance?" Gerald asked.

"For sure, we'll be there," Rhonda replied, glancing at Tyrone who was now reading the sports section of the newspaper.

"What are you going to wear?" Jalani asked Rhonda.

"I don't know yet. Maybe I can get something new. Something that will turn Tyrone upside down."

"Don't be doing that to me!" Tyrone said, looking up from the paper. "That's unfair ammunition against a weak and helpless dude like myself!"

"Helpless, my foot! I'm gonna look like a stone fox!" Rhonda pranced around the kitchen like she was modeling.

"I thought you liked me!" Tyrone pretended to cover his eyes.

"I do!" Rhonda replied. "That's why I want to look like dynamite next week."

Gerald laughed on the phone line, listening to them tease each other. He hung up, promising to call Jalani as soon as she got home.

Jalani and I left shortly after that, with promises to fix Rhonda's hair for the dance. She drove me home because my mom was using my car.

"So, you and Gerald are gettin' tight?" I began.

"Oh, yeah," she said, smiling. "Getting to know Gerald is like digging for treasure. There's so many levels of him to discover. He's like a chocolate cake with a million layers—delicious!"

I was silently hoping that I could find out that much about Jonathan, and hoping I'd get to enjoy every single layer. "Tell me what you figured out about him," I asked her.

"Well, just last week I found out he could draw—roses so real they looked like photographs. 'Why didn't you tell me you could do that?' I asked him. 'You never asked,' he replied simply."

"Sweet," I said.

"Another time I discovered that he knew the name of every single tree we passed, whether we were at a park or walking down the street. I asked him how he learned all that and he told me that he used to go every week to Spring Grove Cemetery to visit his aunt, who died on his ninth birthday. The trees there are labeled. He'd just walk around to clear his thoughts, and look at the trees. 'It just kinda seeped into my brain,' he told me."

"Gerald's cool," I said. "You're lucky."

"He's so much fun to be with. He makes me laugh. And Angel has sorta become like a little sister to me. What about you,

166

Keisha? You gettin' it together?"

"I'm tryin'. I decided to go to the dance after all."

"Really? You got a date?" Jalani seemed to be pleased. "You been keepin' to yourself too much. I've only known you a little while, but I know you gotta get out sometimes and let it hang loose."

I laughed. "You sound like you don't think I can get a date!"

"No, I just wondered who you had decided to go with."

"Nobody." I replied with a hint of mystery in my voice. "That way I can dance with whoever I please!"

"Like Jonathan Hathaway?"

"So what if I do?" I replied defensively.

Jalani ignored my tone of voice. "He scares me, Keisha. There's something not quite right about that dude."

"He seems pretty close to perfect to me," I countered. I thought again about his passionate kiss at the park.

"That's what bothers me," Jalani tried to explain. "He's a little too slick on the edges. His smile always seems pasted on."

"That's 'cause you don't really know him," I declared, defending him. "He's so smart. And he's funny. He makes me laugh. I haven't laughed like that since way before Andy died."

"I know," Jalani said gently. "I'm glad he makes you happy. But don't jump into the deep end, Keisha."

I didn't want to hear what Jalani was saying, what my inner voice, which I had managed to silence, had said to me as well. "In just a few months," I told Jalani, "I'll be a college student. My parents won't be able to say anything, and I won't have to sneak to see Jonathan or anybody else."

"Sounds like you got it all figured out," Jalani replied, sensing my anger.

"Not really," I told her. "I just want to be happy like you and Gerald."

Jalani was quiet for a moment. Then she told me, "There's an old Ibo saying: 'Beware of the gift wrapped with silence. The snake hides under a silver moon.'"

Her words made me shiver, but I refused to let Jalani know. "I'll be careful, Jalani. I'm a big girl. I can take care of myself. What could possibly happen?"

"Has he ever told you he cared about you?" Jalani asked instead of answering my question.

"Well, no, not exactly," I stammered. "But I can tell by the way he looks at me and touches me and talks to me. He told me he thought that I was very mature and very special. He calls me his butterfly!" I smiled with pleasure as I remembered.

"I could say the same thing about a bug stuck with a pin in an insect display," Jalani countered. "Just keep your eyes open, okay?"

"I'll be fine. I can't wait for graduation! Thanks for the ride home." After she dropped me off at my house, I made myself a snack and waited for Jonathan to call.

When the phone rang, I picked it up on the first ring. "Hello?" I said, trying to make my voice sound sexy and mature.

"May I speak to Keisha?" It wasn't Jonathan's voice.

"Speaking," I replied, disappointed. I returned my voice to normal.

"This is Leon. What's up?"

"Just finishing my homework. What's up with you?" I relaxed and glanced at my math book while I sat on my bedroom floor.

"Well, since there are no more dragons to slay or unicorns to capture, I just have to do ordinary stuff like finish reading *Macbeth*. That dude had some serious issues!"

"You got that right!" I laughed.

"Hey Keisha, I guess you already have a date for the Valentine Dance, right?"

"Not really. I was just going to go by myself."

I could hear Leon taking a deep breath. "You want to go with me? I promise I won't stick anything in my nose or ears all evening!"

I thought of my secret date with Jonathan

after the dance, and how going with Leon would make it easy for my parents to let me stay out late. So I said, "That sounds like fun, Leon. They're having a dance contest. I heard you were dynamite on the dance floor!"

I think he was shocked that I agreed so quickly. He had probably expected me to make excuses. He stammered, "That's what some say. I bet we could win it."

"Hey, I can dance, but I'm no Judith Jamison!" I told him. "Now Angel, Gerald's little sister—that girl can move! You gotta check her out."

"That sounds cool, but it's *you* that I wanna dance with!" he managed to say.

"I'm looking forward to it, Leon," I told him, then I said good night and hung up the phone. For sure I was looking forward to that night. I felt a little guilty that I was using Leon, but the thought of Jonathan seeing me all dressed up, and maybe even dancing with me—that made all those negative thoughts float away.

15

The Valentine Dance was second only to prom in importance. We jokingly called it prom practice. Dates were lined up for the prom in May depending on what happened and who it happened with at the Valentine Dance in February. This one wasn't formal, however. Dressy casual, we girls called it. Leather, slacks, or silk. Something new to show off, whether a new outfit or a new date. Brand-name hookups looking obvious, yet understated. Hair done perfectly, shoes just right—a night to remember.

The Valentine Dance was also one that all grades could attend, not like the prom, which was reserved for juniors and seniors. Joyelle and Angel told me they had stood in line after school the very first day the tickets had gone on sale, anxious to be sure they had them in time. Neither girl had a date, but they probably had their eyes on a couple of the unattached sophomore and junior boys who would be there as well, so they planned their outfits down to the exact color of the nail polish they would wear.

My parents were overjoyed that I wanted to go to the dance with Leon, a high school boy who didn't make them feel threatened. He stopped by my house the night before the dance to drop off a Valentine's Day card for me. It was funny, with a fire-breathing dragon on a front, pleading with the lady dragon, who held a giant fire extinguisher, to be his lady love. I laughed, introduced Leon to my parents, who liked him as soon as he walked in the front door. Mom chatted about her job, Dad showed him his new fishing reel, and I thought only of Jonathan the entire time.

When he left, Mom asked, "Where has that one been all this time? He's not bad."

"Oh, Mom, he's just a friend. That's just Leon. It's not like a real date. Leon is just fun to hang with. You know how it is."

"Well, I'm glad you've decided to rejoin high school for these last few months. I like this Leon kid, even if he is just a friend. What time is the dance over?"

The dance was over at midnight, but I

told my mother, "It's over at one." That way, I knew Mom wouldn't be expecting me until at least three or three-thirty. That gave me more time to be with Jonathan. "Then we'll probably go to Waffle House to eat. Or we might go to a movie. I don't know. Just me and Leon and Rhonda and Tyrone, and probably Gerald and Jalani, too. Is that okay?" I knew it would be.

"That sounds like fun. I'm glad you've got friends to hang with. You need to laugh more. Stay out as late as seems reasonable, but remember to call me on your cell phone to check in every once in a while, okay?"

"I will, Mom." I leaned over and kissed her. I couldn't believe how easy this was going to be. I only felt a little guilty about deceiving her.

The next night Leon arrived dressed in black silk slacks and shirt. When I answered the door, he stood there looking excited and nervous. Even though most of the girls would probably be wearing slacks and a casual shirt, I decided to wear a short silver dress, not dressy, but classy and sleek. It had a V-neck front, tie back, and slim cut. Around my neck I wore the silver butterfly necklace.

"You look good, Keisha—that silver really makes you . . . <u>shine</u>," Leon managed to say. "I hope that doesn't sound dumb."

"I like your outfit, too," I told him honestly. I could see his muscles under his shirt and noticed with pleasure how really good he looked. In a couple of years when he's outgrown his high school immaturity, I thought, he'll be dynamite. Mom snapped pictures like cameras were going out of business the next day, but I just smiled and let her take as many as she wanted.

Leon finally led me to his car, after Mom insisted that I take an extra jacket, and we both laughed as we sped down the street to the hall where the dance was being held.

"Is your mother always that nice?" Leon asked.

"No, she can be a real pain when she wants to be," I told him, "but you're lucky—she likes you!"

Leon laughed and relaxed noticeably as we drove. The air was very cold, but clear. Silver stars glittered in the sky. Leon kept grinning at me, and I smiled back, but my smile was really for Jonathan.

We got to the dance, where the music was loud and the crowd was already mixing it up on the dance floor. Joyelle and Angel sat giggling near the potato chips, not dancing, but looking like they were really glad to be there. Gerald, who kept his eye on Angel, danced with Jalani, who wore a copy of a designer outfit that she had seen on the cover of *Vogue*. She looked better than the model who had worn it.

I saw Rhonda, who saw my dress and screamed, "Girl, that dress is the bomb!" Rhonda wore white silk sweats which Tyrone said looked as dynamite as she had promised. Leon stood to one side, seeming to enjoy it all.

I glanced around the room, looking for Jonathan, but I didn't see him in the crowd. I danced with Leon, then Tyrone, Gerald, and even B. J., who didn't bring a date. I was having a good time, but only half my mind was concentrating on the dance. The rest of me searched for Jonathan in the corners of the room.

B. J. casually walked over to where I stood with Angel and Joyelle, who were watching the others dance. Angel wore a long, slim dress which made her look fragile—like a bendable straw. Joyelle, who had slimmed down a bit, looked comfortable in her jeans and sparkle tank top. "You want to dance?" B. J. asked Joyelle.

She looked up in surprise. "Me?" she asked.

"Yeah," he said casually. "I know Angel can dance. That's all Gerald talks about. Let's see what *you* can do!"

"Go on," Angel encouraged her, giggling. "Dance with him!"

"Do it, girl!" I said, giving her a little push.

Joyelle took B. J.'s hand and they danced the next three dances together. Angel watched with excitement. The fourth dance was a slow number, and I was dancing with Leon. B. J. looked like he was dancing in heaven, but I guess Joyelle couldn't take the intensity. She pretended to be tired and out of breath and went to sit down.

"Why didn't you keep on dancing? Punk out?" I heard Angel say.

"You got it!" Joyelle replied. "I need a soda to cool off!"

When Jalani went with Rhonda to the bathroom, Gerald danced with Angel. Watching her move was like looking at a breeze through the trees. Gerald grinned as he complimented her. "You're good, girl!"

"I know!" she teased him. She didn't really need a partner—she moved with the music. Tyrone danced with her a couple of dances; so did B. J. and a couple of boys she didn't even know. She told me that she had never had so much fun.

Everybody in the room jammed the floor for the stomp dances. Angel and Joyelle joined all of us while we let the music take us way beyond the gym.

Just then the DJ announced "Dance Contest—Swing Dance!" Leon glanced at me, and said, "Let's win this thing, Keisha!"

But I had just seen Jonathan walk in the door, so I said, "Ask Angel instead. She's probably the best dancer in this room—including you!" Leon probably thought I was showing sensitivity to Angel—I just wanted to get rid of him for a few minutes.

So Leon said to Angel, "I hear you're the best dancer in the room."

She answered shyly, "I like to dance, but I don't know how good I am."

"You want to be my partner for the swing dance contest?" he asked her.

Surprised, Angel asked, "What about Keisha?"

Leon grinned and said, "No, kid, this one's for you." I nodded at her to go ahead and she and Leon glided on to the dance floor. Nineties kids dancing to forties music. The teachers loved it. Angel and Leon moved to the center of the floor and stayed there, winning round after round. The crowd cheered as Angel and Leon danced in the spotlight spinning and twisting. Angel was light on her feet and seemed to move as if the music flowed through her. Leon, instead of the falls and rolls and slapstick comedy he usually did in the halls at school, used his body to move with the music and dance with style. They were perfect dance partners. While they danced, I hid in the noise and confusion and moved around to the other side of the room where Jonathan stood, not far from his father.

"Hello, Mr. Hathaway," I said to the principal, but Jonathan knew the greeting was for him.

"Well, good evening Keisha, you look magnificent, my dear. That silver really becomes you. Don't you think so, Jonathan?" he said to his son a bit distractedly. He was watching the swing dance competition.

"Oh, of course," Jonathan said quickly, pretending to have just noticed me. But he had watched me approach, had glanced with a nod of approval as I got closer, and I knew that he liked what he saw.

"I'm going to watch the dance contest," Mr. Hathaway told Jonathan and me. "That little freshman, Angel, is quite a dancer! Wow, look at that!" Mr. Hathaway loved the Valentine Dance. He left Jonathan and me standing there in the shadows to watch the dancers.

"You look beautiful," Jonathan said sincerely.

"Thank you," I murmured. My heart was pounding.

"I especially like the butterfly necklace. It's just perfect!"

I was about to thank him for giving it to me, when a great cheer went up and Angel and Leon were announced as finalists in the dance contest. Instead I said quickly, "Are we still going out to eat tonight?"

"Oh, yes," he said. "I'll follow you home, and as soon as I see your date leave, I'll whisk you off to a place where dreams come true."

I looked away from him and toward the crowd that surrounded Angel and Leon. I tried not to show the giddy excitement I felt. "Do we have time for that dance you promised me?" I asked shyly.

"It's probably not a good idea," he answered, glancing around. "Let's save our dance for tonight when we can be alone, okay?"

I nodded and smiled at him with anticipation. "See you soon," I whispered quickly. I hurried back to where Leon and Angel, sweaty but triumphant, held the trophy for winning the dance contest. Gerald made Angel sit down and eat some pizza and drink two glasses of water. She fussed, but she ate it all.

"I'm taking you home," he told her. "Joyelle, you ready to go? Your mom told me to get you home early."

Joyelle nodded, but glanced back at B. J. He waved and grinned at her. "You got it together, Joyelle! We'll have to do this again when your mama will let you stay out after midnight!" She laughed as she found her coat and Angel's and they left with Gerald.

I put my hand to my head and told Leon, "I knew you were good, but you were really something else out there!" I frowned as if my head was hurting.

"It should have been you dancing with me," Leon complained mildly. "Even though we won the contest, I would have much rather danced with you and lost."

"I can't dance like Angel," I told him. "Besides, my head is killing me. I think I'm coming down with something. Can you just take me home?" I rubbed my temples and made my face look like I was in real pain.

"You don't want to go out to eat or anything?" Leon asked me. I could see he was really disappointed.

"Not this time," I replied. I was starting to feel a little guilty. "Maybe we can do something this weekend," I added, trying to give him a little hope.

It worked. He looked fairly cheerful as he found my coat and we headed for the door. I noticed that Jonathan was already wearing his black leather coat as he stood by the door, saying good-bye to the couples leaving early.

Leon inhaled deeply the cold night air. "It's been a good night," he said. "Even with a headache, Keisha, you look like a princess."

"Yeah, it was awesome," I told him. But I thought only of Jonathan. I noticed him in the dark parking lot moving silently to his car and I relaxed, knowing he'd be there.

When we got to my house, Leon walked around to let me out of his car. He grinned like a puppy as he walked me up to the door, did *not* slip on the ice on the sidewalk, and *did* kiss me quickly on the lips before I hurriedly fumbled for my door key. I smiled and whispered to him, "I had fun, Leon. I really did. Call me tomorrow, okay?" I knew that asking him to call me was a signal that I was interested, but I had to get rid of him in a hurry. It worked, and he slid on the ice, on purpose, all the way to his car. I laughed and opened my front door, waved, and watched him drive away.

My house was dark and silent. On the table by the front door was a note:

> Keisha,
> Dad and I went to the movies. We'll probably be home before you will! Call me!
>
> Love, Mom.

"Perfect!" I cheered. "They're not home!" I scribbled a note in reply.

> I came home to change clothes, Mom. We're going out to eat! I'll call you.
>
> Love, Keisha

I didn't say who "we" was, and I had no intention of changing the silver dress that Jonathan obviously liked so much, but now I knew I had several hours before I had to be back home. I rushed back outside, stepped carefully over the ice that Leon had so much fun sliding on, and slipped quickly into the open door of Jonathan's car.

16

"**Relax,**" **was the first** thing Jonathan said in that smooth, soothing voice of his. I wasn't really aware that I had been holding my breath, but I exhaled slowly and sighed with contentment. I looked at him with a grateful smile as he drove through the frosty night. It had started to snow. Huge flakes floated down, covering the streets and trees with magic.

"Where are we going?" I asked finally. "I'm a little hungry after all that dancing." I glanced out of the tinted windows of the Cherokee, watching the streets change from the brightly lit business sections of the city to more dimly lit neighborhoods. "I'm not familiar with all the restaurants in town," I said hesitantly, "but this looks like a residential area."

"Do you doubt me?" he asked, a hint of a chill in his voice.

"I'm sorry," I said quickly. "I was just wondering." I felt stupid.

"We're almost there," he said, his voice returning to its usual mellow tone. "Just relax." He turned the music up, and drove skillfully, in spite of the increasing snowfall, through the narrow streets of the area of town called Mount Adams. The streets were on steep hills, with ritzy apartments and condos overlooking the rest of the city. I closed my eyes and almost dozed, not noticing where we were going. Jonathan pulled into a narrow driveway and turned off the motor. I sat up and looked around. Apartment buildings lined both sides of the narrow street, which I didn't recognize. Several inches of fresh snow had already fallen. The view of the city we had seen from the park was in the distance. "Dinner is served," Jonathan said elaborately, as he came around to open my door. He bowed for me as I stepped out of the car, and I giggled with delight.

"Where's the restaurant?" I asked, stepping carefully through the fresh snow.

"Right up these steps," Jonathan replied, as he opened one of the narrow doors of the building.

"Smells wonderful," I commented. As we

climbed the steps, I wondered how a restaurant could manage in a place like this. But I knew these little places in Mt. Adams thrived on college kids and the newly rich slicks who lived in these condos. *Wait till I tell Rhonda and Jalani about this one,* I thought with pleasure. *And they're eating the same stupid waffles they order every Saturday night!*

At the top of the stairs, Jonathan opened the first door on the left and I was stunned. This was no restaurant—this was Jonathan's apartment! *How stupid could I be,* I thought, wishing I could kick myself. To Jonathan I said, "Why didn't you just tell me you were taking me to your apartment?" I stepped inside the door warily.

"I wanted to surprise you!" he said simply. The hurt and disappointment on his face made me sorry I had used that tone of voice with him. "We'll leave if you feel uncomfortable," he offered.

Again, I found myself apologizing to him. "I'm sorry, Jonathan, but this is just a little unusual. I was expecting a real restaurant, you know."

"I know, but look what I have prepared for you. I've been working all day." He touched a light switch and the room was glowing with soft lights and soft music. The faint smell of lavender seemed to float on the air. While I stood there, a little overwhelmed with the scene, Jonathan walked around the living room and lit candles. Lavender. They burned low on the corner tables.

"It's lovely," I said honestly. "I've only seen places like this in movies." I felt a little uncomfortable, but Jonathan was acting like such a gentleman, and seemed to be trying so hard to please me that it was difficult to be angry. It was actually kinda exciting.

The living room was small, with a soft beige sofa, two wicker chairs, and a coffee table made of petrified wood. Over the sofa, instead of the usual piece of art, a huge framed mirror dominated the wall. Jonathan glanced at it as he was lighting the candles and noticed a tiny piece of lint on his gray silk shirt. He flicked it away. Smaller tables in the corners of the room held the candles and bits of decorative artwork. He had set up the far end of the room as a dining area, with a small table covered with white linen and two wooden chairs. The dinner table was set for two with wine glasses, crystal goblets, and fine china. The room was simple but charming—a room decorated by a man with taste, I thought. The tiny kitchen was off to the left, his bedroom to the right.

I wasn't sure what to do or where to sit. I glanced at my watch.

"Let's eat," he said, noticing me check the time. "We only have a few brief moments together. Please sit down." He opened the oven and brought out two perfectly cooked Cornish hens, brown rice, broccoli, and soft, warm rolls.

"When did you do all this?" I asked in admiration and amazement.

"I would tell you I cooked it," he told me as he set the food on the table in front of me. "But I won't lie. I ordered it from a gourmet company that delivered it just a couple of hours ago. That's why I was late to the dance."

"I started to think you weren't coming," I said, putting my napkin in my lap.

"All I have thought about today is you," he replied, looking directly at me with his strangely golden eyes. I blushed again.

He brought out a bottle of what looked like red wine. I was trying to figure out how I was going to refuse the wine without sounding like a kid, when he showed me the label. "Non-alcoholic—just for you," he said with a smile.

I sighed with relief. The drink was fresh and cold and strongly carbonated. It was delicious. By the time we finished dinner, I had relaxed enough to feel comfortable in his place. I explored his rock collection and his collection of coins from around the world. I glanced at his bedroom, but decided not to even go in there. He noticed my nervousness and quickly closed his bedroom door. I was really pleased to note his concern for my feelings. He's trying so hard to show me an adult evening, I thought. I really liked feeling so grown and mature.

I walked around the small living room, lighting more candles, looking at the tiny mementos that he had collected from around the world. He had a delicate Italian vase, a hand-carved German mug, a tiny French sculpture, and a Spanish bullfighting cape. I was aware that he was watching me, admiring my silver dress. We ended up on the sofa in the living room, laughing at his photo albums: pictures of Jonathan as an infant in Italy, a small boy in Germany, and a gawky twelve-year-old in Spain. From the time he was small, he was extremely good-looking, but in none of the pictures was he smiling. I also noticed, but did not mention, that there were no pictures of his mother at all. I found one picture of his father looking dusty and brown in an old Army uniform, and amazingly, just like Jonathan looked now.

I leaned against him and he put his arm around me. I felt safe and alive and very sure of myself. I kicked off my shoes. He fingered the silver butterfly necklace.

"This is very pretty," he murmured, "and so are you."

I smiled. "I've been meaning to thank you. It's so lovely."

"Thank me? Why?" he asked.

"For leaving the necklace on my doorstep on Christmas," I said shyly. "It was the most wonderful gift I ever received."

"I wish I could take credit for it, and I wish I had done something thoughtful like that, but I didn't leave it," Jonathan told me.

"Then what about the flowers—the ones wrapped in the same silver ribbon as the box that had the necklace in it?" I asked in confusion.

"Nope, that wasn't me either," Jonathan told me cheerfully. "You must have a high school admirer—one of those little boys that you've outgrown."

I frowned and tried to think who could possibly have sent me flowers or given me the necklace. I was sure it was the same person. *Leon!* I thought to myself suddenly. *Of course! And he never said anything!* I smiled to myself and made a mental note to be sure to thank Leon tomorrow. *Jonathan is right, though,* I thought. *I'm so much more mature than high school boys like Leon. He's a good friend, but he has no idea how to act like a real man. This is a world that Leon can't even imagine. Dim lights. Candles. Romance.* I breathed with pleasure as Jonathan gently stroked my hair.

Jonathan leaned over and kissed me as the music from the CD throbbed and rolled in the background. At some point Jonathan had turned down most of the lights in the room—the only light came from the lavender-scented candles. I sighed with contentment and let him kiss me again. This time his kiss was more demanding and he squeezed my arm so hard it hurt. I had to push him back so I could sit up on the couch. "Hey!" I cried out. "You're hurting me!" I rubbed my arm and frowned.

It was Jonathan's turn to apologize. He inched closer to me. I could feel the warmth of his leg next to mine. "I'm sorry, Keisha," he murmured into my ear. "But you look so good in that dress, I can't help myself. Please forgive me."

I glanced at my watch again. "I probably should be heading home now, Jonathan," I suggested. "This has been such a wonderful evening. I want it to end at a place where I can remember it with pleasure forever." I glanced out of the window and noticed that the snow had steadily continued to fall.

"You're right," Jonathan agreed. "I just want to remember you and how delicate and lovely you . . ." He never finished the sentence for he kissed me again, gently this time, slowly erasing my defenses just as smoothly as the teacher erased the chalk off the board at school. I felt myself fading again, but one level of my mind felt real fear—fear that I was in a situation way over my head. He kissed my ear, then the silver necklace on my neck, the fierce intensity returning as he held me much too tightly. His hands began to roam. Suddenly I didn't feel like much of a grown-up. I was getting scared and I had no idea how to make him stop, except to say so.

"No! Stop!" I said forcefully. "You're moving too fast, Jonathan. I think you better take me home now." I pushed him away once more and jumped up from the sofa, trying to smooth my hair with my hands and smooth the wrinkles from my dress. I didn't want him to think I was being impolite—after all, he had gone out of his way to make that great surprise dinner for me. Maybe I was overreacting.

Jonathan simply smiled. He held out his hand. "Come and sit down, Keisha. You're trembling." It was true. I was shaking with fear. "I promise I'll behave myself," he said apologetically. He extended his hand again.

But instead of reaching out toward him, I backed slowly away from him. I glanced nervously around his apartment, trying to peer through the smoky light, looking for something, anything that might help me. I could see my dim reflection in the huge wall mirror. My eyes were full of fear. Jonathan got up from the sofa. He never took his eyes from me. He walked toward me. Slowly I continued to back up toward the door. When I reached the door, I could go no further. I reached for the doorknob behind me and turned.

Nothing happened. The door was locked.

"Why do you want to leave so soon?" he murmured in that buttery smooth voice. "You were just beginning to relax and feel comfortable."

"I want to go home, Jonathan," I said firmly. "I'm not ready for this. And I don't feel comfortable at all right now. You've never acted like this before!"

"And you've never acted like a stupid high school kid before!" he snapped back at me. "I thought you were different—more mature. Why'd you wear that skimpy little silver dress if you didn't want to be treated like a woman?"

I reeled as if I'd been slapped. I wasn't sure how to respond. "I'm . . . I'm sorry," I stammered, although I didn't know what I was apologizing for. "Can you just unlock the door? We can talk about this tomorrow." I was about to cry.

"Don't cry, Keisha," Jonathan murmured gently. He reached out for me and wrapped his arms around me, pushing me against the locked door. His embrace wasn't gentle, however. When I tried to pull away, I found he had me pinned to the door with his body. I couldn't move. He tried to kiss me again, harshly this time, but I twisted my face away. I could feel the stubble of his beard as it scratched my face and I fought to free myself.

I tried frantically to remember what I'd read about self-defense in these situations. I had slept through this chapter in health class, thinking it boring and unnecessary. What was it? Kick him? Scratch him? Spray mace? All of that seemed foolish and futile now.

"*Stop!*" I screamed as I gathered all my strength and pushed him away from me. I took the moment to duck away from him, trying to find a place to run in the dimly lit room. He lunged after me, grabbing the back of my dress, which ripped as I pulled away from him. I jumped on the sofa, then on the table, knocking over the wineglasses. "Don't touch me! Let me out of here!"

"I told you to just relax!" he repeated. "Quit acting like such a baby!"

I was terrified. I no longer felt like an adult. I felt like a child who had jumped into the deep end of the pool and I needed help, quickly. I wanted my mom, my dad, daylight— anything to get me away from this golden-eyed creature who held me against my will. "*No!*" I screamed. "*No!* Leave me alone!" I ran behind the sofa, grabbing a wine bottle from the table.

"Grow up, Keisha," Jonathan snarled. Gone was his smooth, mellow voice and his gentle attitude.

"*No!*" I yelled again. I threw the empty bottle at him. He ducked it easily, laughing. I tried to reason with him as I ran from corner to corner of the small apartment. "If you do this, I swear I will tell!" I warned. "You'll lose your job, your dad will lose his job, you'll go to jail, and . . ."

"I couldn't care less about my father," Jonathan said harshly, interrupting me.

I couldn't think of anything else to threaten him with. I was breathing hard and trying not to give in to the hysteria I felt.

He had calmed down a bit, and he looked at me coolly. He was once again in control. "And you'll tell what?" he jeered. "That you came over here alone in that sexy little silver dress? That you sneaked out of the house and lied to your parents to be with me? That you kissed me like a woman kisses a man, not like a high school girl kisses a boy? Is that what you want to tell?"

I wept real tears then for I knew he was right. He would walk away unpunished.

"You'll look like a fool if this ever gets out," he told me. His voice was slow and manipulating. "All your friends, all your teachers will know what you have done. Your parents will look at you in disgust." He smiled as he watched me cry. "It will be all your fault, you know."

Jonathan glanced at himself in the mirror above the sofa. He smoothed his hair a bit, smiled, and watched himself walk toward me.

I stood trembling behind the chair. Terrified, I ran once more to the door, screaming for help and fruitlessly rattling the locked doorknob.

"*Help!*" I screamed. "Somebody, please help me!" I screamed as loud as I could and pounded on the door praying that someone, anyone would hear me. No one did.

He grabbed my shoulder, spun me around to face him, then reached into his pants pocket and took out the key to the inside door lock. He laughed and tossed it on the floor. "You won't be needing this," he said softly.

Still crying, I spit in his face. "Unlock the door, you pervert!"

Jonathan never took his eyes from me. He calmly wiped off his face, then reached into his pocket once more. This time he brought out a small, silver-handled knife. It gleamed with sharp intention in the darkness. I felt its sharp pointed tip at my neck. "Silence!" he said quietly. "Do as I say and you won't get hurt. Relax. That's what I've been telling you all evening. Just relax." The soothing voice was back, but his tone was harsh and cruel.

Crying and trembling, I tried once more to kick him and lunge away, but I felt the knife point pierce my neck. I cried out as a small drop of blood joined the point of the knife and rolled down the length of the silver necklace. "Just relax," he said again. "If you fight me again," he warned me viciously, "I will have to hurt you."

"Well, you're just going to have to hurt me!" I screamed as I twisted my body and pushed him off balance. "But you are *not* man enough to handle me!" I spoke with a confidence that I really didn't feel. He hesitated for just a second before he tried to grab my arm. I used that second to lunge for the knife and grab it from him.

He laughed, grabbed my wrist, and tried to twist the knife away from me. But that wasn't so easy. I screamed and gripped it firmly, moving with him in a horrible sort of dance as he tried to make the knife his once more. He pulled my arm over my head, right at the level of his face, and squeezed my wrist to make me release it. But I held on, closing my eyes and pulling my arm back down with all my strength, down to my waist, and around in back of me.

I opened my eyes when I heard *him* scream, and suddenly he let me go. In trying to get away from him, I had pulled the knife down right across his face. A huge bright red diagonal slice from the top of his hairline, across his left eye, past his nose, and across his lips to his chin marred his once-perfect face. My eyes widened in horror as I saw what I had done. He held his face in his hands, groaning.

I dropped the knife as if it were made of fire, looked quickly to the floor, located the key, and had the door open in a second. I had no time to find my coat or shoes or purse. I ran barefoot down the stairs out of the building and into the fifteen-degree night wearing only my torn silver dress.

17

It was snowing heavily and I was alone. Large white flakes seemed to pour from the sky, making the street lights look fuzzy and silvery. Snow fell on my bare back and arms and down my dress. My bare feet sank into the newly fallen snow, burning and freezing them at the same time. I wasn't sure where I was, what time it was, or where to go. My trembling increased—my brain wouldn't work. I had no idea what to do. I thought vaguely that I should try to find a pay phone, but I couldn't see one in either direction of the dimly lit street, and the thought passed as I shivered violently in the darkness. No lights could be seen in any of the windows, no cars moved on the narrow streets. A strong gust of wind blasted me, pelting me with more snow, freezing even my eyelashes with ice, reminding me that I was almost naked and in need of help in a hurry. I rang the doorbells of every building that I could find with one, but no one answered. Fifteen minutes passed. I tried banging on several doors of other buildings I passed, but all were locked, dark, and snow-covered. I knew thirty or forty minutes had passed, and still not one single car had driven down that street. I wandered down the street, trying to think, but it was so cold. My brain felt like frozen mud. I tried to force myself to go on, but my mind seemed to freeze along with my body, and I collapsed by a mailbox near the corner, unable to move any longer. I guess I faded into unconsciousness. All I remember is the snow, which continued to fall, silent and silver.

"What you doin' out here, girlie, 'sides freezin' to death?" The old woman shuffled closer and gently kicked my bare leg. "Hey! You dead or alive?" I heard her from what seemed like a great distance.

"Help me," I managed to say before I faded away once more.

The woman, who was wrapped in several coats and shawls, removed one of her coats. I vaguely remember that she wrapped it around my body, and lifted me effortlessly into her arms. She walked down the block, turned into an alley, and disappeared into a basement door. The building was warm, and I stirred as the heat from the coat and the furnace that filled most of that basement began to warm me. The woman set me gently on an old mattress in the corner and covered me with another coat. I opened my eyes slowly. At first I looked around with fear, then I saw the kindly eyes of a strange old woman. She looked vaguely familiar. I relaxed and I guess I passed out again.

When I woke up, the woman was gently bathing my swollen and icy feet, massaging them back into circulation. She carefully washed my wounds—the cut on my neck, the bruises on my arms. It felt good. I dozed a little, so grateful for the kind touches, the soft words.

The old woman dug around in the bottom of one of the many cardboard boxes lined against the walls of the basement. She pulled out a clean, green plaid sweatshirt that said SMILE! GOD LOVES YOU on the front. She said it was one of many given to her at church clothing drives. Then she found a clean pair of bright orange sweatpants. "They don't give away the clothes that match, sweetie," she mumbled. The woman gently and carefully slipped the shirt and pants on me.

"You gonna need more healin' than I can give ya, poor baby," the old woman muttered.

Suddenly I jerked in fear, startled by the noise of the furnace kicking on.

"Don't fret none about that, child. It's just the furnace doin' its thing and givin' more heat to the folks upstairs. But we got plenty down here, and ol' Edna gonna take care of you. Don't you fret now, you hear? You been through enough tonight."

"Edna! I remember you!"

"And I remember you, too, chile. I been all over this city and this is the first time I ever found a half-froze girl on the street!" She laughed a little and showed several missing teeth. "But you just rest now—and let Edna work."

I wasn't scared. I lay quietly, glancing over at Edna. She wasn't really that old—maybe sixty or so. Her face was worn and brown, wrinkled like a walnut. Her clothes were old, but her eyes were bright with kindness.

"Where am I?" I asked.

"Not far from where I found you. Probably not far from whatever building you wandered out of. Or got tossed out of. You remember leaving a building around here? You live around here?"

I was silent, for remembering was painful. "No, I don't live around here," I replied, half answering the question.

"What's your name, honey?" Edna asked me. "I forget."

I sneezed.

Edna laughed and said, "I remember now! You the girl whose name sounds like a sneeze! Katchoo or something."

I smiled and told her, "It's Keisha. Keisha Montgomery." But somehow, hearing my name said out loud made reality return. I began to cry once more—deep, wracking sobs that wouldn't stop. Edna held me in her arms and let me cry, asking no questions.

"You want some soup, baby? Edna's got some nice warm broth. Make you feel better inside." I nodded and gratefully sipped the hot soup out of what looked like it might have once been a flower pot.

"You know, one day, not too long ago, old Edna was hungry. It was just before Christmas, and before I found this great place here. Two girls stopped and gave me some soup. Best soup I ever done had. I'll never forget that. Pretty girls. Pretty names," she added, since she had teased me about my name. "Pretty nice."

I smiled at her. "I'm glad we stopped that day."

"Lawdy me," Edna replied, "Ol' Edna don't often get to repay a favor—feels real good. Now, that's a purty smile if I ever seen one," Edna told me.

"I didn't think I would ever smile again," I

said sadly. I thought about the horrible night with Jonathan.

"You gotta smile, baby. Smilin' is the medicine God give us to heal us from pain. You gonna get over this. You gonna smile for the rest of your life."

"Can't I stay here with you?" I asked desperately. "It's safe here. I can't . . . I can't *tell* anybody! I can't even *look* at anybody! They'll know how stupid I was!" I started crying again.

"What you want to do a fool thing like stay here with ol' Edna? They be chasin' me outta here by next week. You got a life, child. You gotta go live it."

"I don't have a life anymore," I murmured. I shuddered and held Edna's old coat tightly around me. "He ruined it."

"You don't look dead to me!" Edna said sharply. "He didn't take yo' life, girl. All he took was a little piece of your shell. I done had pieces of my shell plucked all my life, but can't *nobody* take away my spirit!" Edna jumped up and did a little dance. She was a sight, with her mismatched boots, her layers of coats and scarves, and her two hats, dancing on the bare floor of the basement, the only light coming from the furnace grate. "Hallelujah! Praise the Lord! Life is good!" Edna declared with a smile.

"But how can you be so happy?" I asked. "Your life looks like it's pretty rough."

"Oh, it is, baby. It is. But I got a powerful spirit, and sometimes I get to share it with somebody special like you. I think I was guided to you tonight."

"You saved my life," I told her gratefully.

"No, child. You saved your own life. I just patched up your body and put a bandage on your soul. You gonna be just fine. Now, don't you think you ought to call your mama?"

I nodded, then looked up helplessly. "I left my purse, my phone, even my shoes," I said with shame. "Thank you for . . ." I glanced down at the bright orange sweatpants and the green plaid sweatshirt with the happy face grinning stupidly.

"For what the church lady didn't want?" Edna laughed.

I smiled a little as well at the foolish outfit. "What should I tell my mother?" I wailed then.

"The truth!" Edna said emphatically. "Yo' mama loves you. She's probably lookin' for you right now. She'll forgive whatever needs forgivin', and she'll help with whatever you need help with. I know. I was a mama once." Edna fell silent.

"What time is it?" I asked, glancing at the empty place on my arm where my watch used to be. I didn't even remember losing it.

Edna pulled back her three coat sleeves and revealed six watches on her left arm. She grinned. "Time in England? Nigeria? Or right here?" I laughed in spite of myself. "Let's see." Edna squinted at the first watch. "It's five A.M. Way past time for girlies like you to be home in bed."

I gasped. "I was supposed to be home hours ago. My mother is going to kill me! I know she's worried sick! But how can I call her? Do you know where the closest pay phone is?"

"Now don't you worry none," Edna replied. She dug around in another cardboard box and pulled out three cellular phones. "I don't steal," she told me quickly, "but I do know how to make a deal with the winos around here. I think this one still got some juice and some air time on it. Call yo' mama." Edna handed me the phone. I was stunned.

"Why didn't you give me this earlier?" I asked as I punched the numbers.

"'Cause you wasn't ready." Edna busied herself in another corner, digging in another of her numerous cardboard boxes.

The phone rang and connected. My mother answered almost immediately. "Hello!" Her voice sounded urgent and worried.

"Mommy. . . ." I began to cry as soon as I heard her voice. "Can you come and get me? I'm in big trouble, and I'm . . . I'm . . . so sorry, Mommy."

18

With directions from Edna, even in spite of the heavy snow, Mom and Dad arrived at Edna's basement refuge in about ten minutes. Slowly, painfully, I told them the whole story, leaving out nothing. I wouldn't leave Edna until I had told them everything. Edna gave me the courage to speak just by being there. Mom hugged me and cried with me. Edna watched silently, feelings of sorrow as well as joy on her face.

Daddy wanted to break something, to hurl a rock at the face of the man who had tried to hurt his daughter. "I told you I didn't like that dude! Maybe now you'll listen to me!" He stomped out of the small basement, cursing and shouting. He wasn't ashamed to show his angry tears. Then he came back down the steps, gratefully thanked Edna, and offered her a large sum of money. She forcefully refused it.

"Next time you see a stinky old homeless person," Edna told him with dignity, "give that wad of money to him! Works better if you give it to a stranger. You git better blessin's that way. I'd like to think of myself as this here chile's friend."

I guess Daddy felt ashamed. "You're right ma'am," he said. "I'm going to be more generous next time I see a person in need. And you truly are her friend. I can never thank you enough."

"You just did," Edna said, winking at him.

He walked back out into the snowy night several times. I could tell he was seething. He kept storming back into the tiny room, breathing hard and curling and uncurling his fists.

"I'm sorry I lied to you, Daddy," I said suddenly. "I thought I was grown and could handle myself in any situation. Oh, Mom, I was so stupid!"

"Many women much older and wiser than you have learned the same terrible lesson, my baby girl," Mom soothed. "It just hurts me to my heart that this had to happen to you! I was so afraid and so worried that something terrible had happened to you. Every mother worries like that when her kids are out at night." She was shaking with anger.

"I'm just glad you were able to get out of there!" Daddy said. "It could have been so much more terrible if . . . " He couldn't even finish the thought.

"When did you start to figure out that something was really wrong?" I asked.

"When we got home from the movie, I saw your note, so initially I wasn't worried," Mom began, wiping her nose on her coat sleeve. "Then, when you hadn't called by two, I started to get angry . . ."

". . . because we had just had a big blow up because of that," I finished for her.

"Your phone didn't even ring—it just gave me a recording. I must have called thirty times, getting angrier and more worried every minute."

"By three we started calling your friends, but all of them said you left the dance early with a headache," Daddy added angrily. "You had them all fooled, too!"

"I'm sorry, Daddy," I said tearfully. "I'm so sorry!"

Mom continued, "So I called Leon's house and he was in bed asleep. He said he brought you home right before midnight, but when he tried to call you after he got home, there was no answer. He just figured you didn't want to talk to him." I hung my head in shame again.

Leon, who had been so kind and so genuine with me, who had given me the lovely silver necklace, I had treated like dirt—dumped him to run off to be with Jonathan.

"He's been all over the city looking for you since I called," my mother added. "He really cares about you, Keisha."

"I know," I said quietly.

"I called the police then," my father told me. "There was very little they could do that we had not already done, but they did check the hospitals and accident reports."

"So when you called, I was frantic!" Mom burst into tears again. "All I could do at that point was pray for your safe return."

"Let's get her out of here," Daddy said suddenly. "We've got to call the police."

"No! Daddy! Not the police!" I burst into tears again. "I just want to go home!"

"The police are already involved," Mom explained. "They need to know that you've been found safely and they have to make a report so that the monster who tried to do this to you can be dealt with properly."

"No!" I screamed. "I don't want anybody to know. I don't want to have to talk about it ever again! Please can we just go home? Please?" I buried my face in my mother's arms.

"I will be right there with you, Keisha," my mother promised. "We'll make this as quick and easy as possible. Then we'll go home. I promise."

"I know it's hard, baby," my father said, choking back tears. "I wish I could take this away from you. I wish I could take you to a place where nothing bad ever happens to Daddy's little girl."

"Will I get in trouble for cutting his face?" I asked fearfully.

"No, dear. Not at all," Mom replied. "You were defending yourself. And I am so glad that you were able to!"

I gave Edna a tearful hug as my parents got ready to leave with me. Edna whispered into my ear, "Yo' spirit is a shinin' silver star, chile. Can't nobody take that away from you. Remember that, you hear?"

"Yes, ma'am," I told her tearfully. "Thank you, Edna." With that, my parents whisked me away. I was silent during the ride to the police station, thinking of Edna's last words: *Yo' spirit is a shinin' silver star, chile. Can't nobody take that away from you.*

When we got there, I had to tell the story again, in slow and graphic detail this time. But the young female police officer who questioned me was patient and gentle, and let me cry when I needed to. In spite of Jonathan's threats, I gave a complete description of him, and how to get in touch with him through his father.

"What will happen to him?" I asked the police officer with dull concern.

"If we find him, he will be arrested, then probably released on bail," the police officer said.

"He'll be allowed to come to school and pretend nothing has happened?" I asked in amazement.

"No, I'll do the follow-up myself to make sure he is not allowed to be within a half mile of any school. He won't be able to bother you or any other girl in that school. I promise," she assured me.

"Will there be a trial?" I asked fearfully. I couldn't bear to have all the personal details about what happened to me showing up on the six o'clock news. I would die of mortification.

The police officer was honest. "If you press charges, if he is indicted, if they feel they have enough evidence to convict him—yes, there could be a trial."

"And if I don't press charges?" I asked her.

"Then he is free to do this again. And again. To other unsuspecting girls."

"Can I go home now?" I asked in desperation. I couldn't handle one more thought. I wanted to think of nothing at all—no fear, no danger—nothing.

When I walked into my house, I glanced at the scribbled lie I had left for my mother.

Everything looked the same in the house, but I knew that nothing would ever be the same again. The long, dark sofa, the picture of the black choir singers on the left wall, the blue carpet—it all seemed to look back at me and mock me. I ran to the shower to wash away the pain and the shame of the night. I felt as if I would never be clean or safe again.

My skin seemed to absorb the needles of hot water, but I never really felt their warmth. My eyes focused on nothing—not the water swirling about me, not my body huddled in the bottom of the shower stall. My thoughts focused on nothing as well. To think would be to remember, and I couldn't bear to remember anymore.

I sat on the floor of the shower, long past the time when the water ran hot, long past the time when the water turned to chilly darts pricking at my skin. I didn't care. When I heard Mom's insistent knocking on the bathroom door, I finally turned off the water, wrapped myself in a towel, and stepped from the shower.

"I'm all right, Mom," I lied. I didn't think I would ever be right again. I shivered fiercely in the chilly bathroom, my hair dripping onto the throw rug beneath my feet. I kept my head down, embarrassed to look at myself in the mirror. I opened the bathroom door, where Mom stood with a towel she had warmed in the dryer. I took it gratefully as I hugged my mother once more.

"Sleep, now, baby girl," Mom said quietly. "Don't think. Don't worry. Just sleep. It's over now. You have come through the fire a stronger and wiser person, I know. Get some sleep. I'll be right here. I will not leave you. I promise."

I could barely stand. I was exhausted. I let my mother lead me down the hall to the pinks and pastels of my bedroom—the soft, comforting bed of my childhood. I collapsed into my pillows and finally slept. I did not dream.

I slept most of the rest of that Sunday, refusing to talk to anyone except my parents. Rhonda called several times, but I wouldn't take the phone. Jalani called, as well as Gerald and B. J. Leon called every hour on the hour, patiently waiting for the chance to talk to me. But I just couldn't. The police called to report that when they arrived at Jonathan's apartment, the doors were unlocked but he was gone. I ate very little, even though Mom fixed special treats to entice me. I faced the wall and kept the world outside of my bedroom.

My father told me that Jonathan had not been at his father's house either when the police went looking for him, nor had he returned to his apartment. The police found plenty of evidence there, however—the broken bottle, my shoes, smeared drops of blood—more than enough to back up my story.

I know it didn't take long for everyone at school to know what had happened. Rhonda told me later that when the police showed up at the home of Mr. Hathaway, a student in the eleventh grade who lived next door to him told her girlfriends what she had seen and overheard. Those girls called several of their friends, who each called several more, so by Monday morning the school was buzzing with rumors and half-truths. Even though I wasn't there, I could imagine exactly what they said.

"You hear about Keisha and Jonathan Hathaway?"

"Yeah. That pig! I knew there was something wrong with him."

"Those funny yellow eyes—like an animal of some kind."

"I thought he was fine!"

"The way I hear it, he ain't fine no more!"

"She sliced him big time!"

"She didn't mean to—she was just tryin' to get away!"

"Yeah, right. She probably tried to mess him up!"

"I'd rather have me an ugly dude who treated me right instead of a pretty boy who did me wrong!"

"Well, she always trying to be Miss Thang! She probably asked for it."

"How you say that? Don't *nobody* ask for nothing like that!"

"If a girls says *no*, that ought to mean *no!*"

"Yeah, you right, but she always wore her skirts so short and her shirts so tight!"

"Look at you, girl. Look at your skirt! Does that mean you lookin' to get raped?"

"I feel you. You right. She didn't deserve that."

"I feel sorry for Keisha. I heard she won't come out of her bedroom."

"Poor kid."

"And for sure she won't come back to school."

"Well, would you?"

"Not with everybody talking about me and knowin' my personal business. I don't blame her."

"She ain't got nothing to be ashamed of! I'm proud of her! Women gotta learn to fight back!"

"Serious mess, girl. Watch yourself."

"Back at you."

"Peace."

And I just couldn't bear it. I refused to go to school, even though I was physically okay, and I refused to talk to anyone on the phone. When my friends came to my house, I locked my bedroom door and ignored their knocks. I know it hurt them, but I couldn't help it. I refused to talk to the police and I wouldn't sign the statement pressing charges. I was supposed to go to group sessions for victims of crime, but I refused to get dressed. I just lay in my bed and faced the wall. Two weeks passed, and I still couldn't move on.

My mother told me that Jonathan Hathaway had disappeared. No one had seen him since that Saturday night. His car was gone, but his clothes and the rest of his belongings remained in the apartment. His picture appeared on the front page of the newspaper, with a reward offered for his arrest. A small story accompanied his picture, but they didn't print my name. Everybody knew, though. I know that everybody knew.

My mother wanted to give me the chance to heal, but I'm sure I was starting to get on her nerves. She called several counseling centers to ask for help and tried suggestions from all of them. She told me that she even drove over to the place where Edna lived to see if she could get her to talk to me, but nothing remained but the furnace and some empty cardboard boxes. Edna had moved on.

On March first, I heard the doorbell ring. I could hear my mother talking to whoever was at the door, probably telling her that I didn't want to see anybody. But soon I heard steps approaching my bedroom door. Whoever it was, I wasn't interested.

"Could I talk to her alone for a few minutes?" I heard the voice say to my mother.

"Sure. I'll be right downstairs if you need me." I know Mom was desperate to find someone who could break through to me.

"Keisha!" the voice called. It was a female voice.

"Go away!" came my muffled reply.

"My name is Rita Bronson. I was on the cross-country team for a while last year. Remember?"

"So what? Go away."

"I was attacked by Jonathan Hathaway also." Her voice was clear and firm. "But I was not as lucky as you were. You got away. I didn't."

I opened the door.

My hair was uncombed, I still wore my pajamas, and my eyes looked sunken and distant. Rita marched into my room, looked at the window blinds, which were closed and let in none of the afternoon sunlight, and checked out my leaden-looking face. Rita took a deep breath, raised her arm suddenly, and slapped my face with a sharp, crisp *whack*. I gasped and cried out in pain and surprise. "Are you crazy?" I shouted as I rubbed my throbbing cheek. "Get out of here! You can't come to somebody's house and just hit them! Who do you think you are? Get out of here!" I was so angry I couldn't even cry.

Rita didn't leave. She sat down on my unmade bed and said, "At least I got your attention. I bet that's the first emotion except for feeling sorry for yourself that you've had since your attack."

I refused to agree with her. "Where do you get off coming in here smacking me around?"

Rita sighed. "I was once where you are, Keisha. I didn't think I could live again. But right now, you are doing exactly what he wants you to do. You are letting him control your life, your thoughts, your very existence. Is that what *you* want?"

I said nothing at first. "How did you find out?"

"Everybody knows, Keisha. Get over it. People care about you and you won't let them help you."

I began to cry. "I'm so ashamed of myself. I'm afraid to face anybody."

"What are *you* ashamed for? You ought to be proud of yourself. You survived. You're alive! You managed to outwit him, overpower him, and escape from him. You ought to be screaming that proudly on national TV instead of hiding in here like you did something wrong. The only way to beat him is to live, and live well!" Rita's eyes flashed with anger.

"Is that what you did?" I asked sullenly.

Rita sighed and picked a piece of lint off the bedspread. "No, I was like you at first. Remember that day at track practice when

Rhonda and Tyrone found me and took me home?"

"Yeah, they said you were upset, but nobody knew what was wrong, and then you didn't come back to school."

"I had been dating Jonathan," Rita began. "Secretly, of course. My mother hated any man I dated, so I kept them a secret."

"How long had you been seeing him?"

"Oh, long before he came to Hazelwood. I guess I met him last summer. He was so smooth and sophisticated—a breath of fresh air for me. He wasn't like the usual trashy men I found myself attracted to. He had class; at least, I thought so."

"I feel you," I said, hanging my head.

"When school started, I went out for cross-country to get myself together. I really wanted to straighten out my life and graduate with the rest of you this year."

"Did you go out for cross-country because he was the coach?" I asked.

"No, actually, he decided to coach the team when he found out I had decided to run. But I think he had already turned his attention to you that first day of school."

"I had no idea," I said quietly.

"I know." Rita sighed. "That's partly why I'm here. I was no sweet little innocent like you. I'd had older boyfriends, and I'd run away from home before. But that didn't make what he did to me any less horrible." She walked over to my window and opened the blinds. She stood there for a moment peering at the afternoon sky.

"Can you talk about it?" I asked.

Rita took a deep breath and began. "He was always such a gentleman. He took me to museums and the opera and the ballet. I had never been to anything like that and I was overwhelmed with the beauty—I guess the word is *maturity*—of it all. I felt like a lady for once in my life."

Tears rolled down my face. "I know exactly what you're saying."

"Finally, the night before Rhonda and Tyrone found me after practice, he invited me to his apartment."

I gasped. "He had wine and soft music and candles, right?"

"Lavender," we said together. We both almost gagged at the thought.

"And a huge mirror," Rita added. "I think he liked looking at himself more than he liked looking at me. He was *so* vain!"

"Now that you mention it, you're right!" I mused. "Even in the car, he constantly checked himself in the rearview mirror. There's something sickening about that."

"Oh, he's a real sick bird," Rita continued. "Anyway, when things got too hot and heavy and I decided I wanted to go home, he dragged me into his bedroom and, well . . . you know. He raped me." Rita was trembling.

I reached over and touched Rita's hand. "Did he have a knife?" I asked.

"A silver-handled, sharp-pointed blade that he kept in his pocket." Both of us were silent, remembering our own personal horror. "He cut me here," Rita said, pointing to a faint, but long and jagged scar on her neck. "I wish I had been able to fight back like you did. He was just too quick and too strong." She started to cry.

I wept also, touching the scab on my neck. "I don't know how I was able to do it. I didn't *mean* to cut him; I didn't even *try* to cut him. I just remember looking up and seeing his face sliced like a piece of meat. It scared me to death." I let myself remember for a moment, then shook the thought away and asked Rita, "So what happened next?"

Rita sighed deeply and continued. "The next day I tried to pretend that it was no big deal. I went to school! Can you believe it? Somehow I thought if I pretended it had never happened that the memory would go away."

"You've got more guts than me," I told Rita. "I haven't been out of my house in two weeks."

"Everybody reacts differently," Rita told me. "I had no one to talk to, so I just stuffed it inside. I even went to practice, where I knew he would be. I don't know what I expected, but somehow I figured he would be nice to me. Stupid, stupid, stupid."

"Don't say that," I said. "You were just trying to cope the best way you knew how. What happened at practice that day?"

"It was awful," Rita began. "He yelled at me and laughed at me. I could see those golden eyes mocking me. When I couldn't take any more, I threatened to tell what he had done to me. Then he threatened to tell what he had done *for* me."

"What do you mean?" I asked, confused.

"My high school years were all messed up. I failed most of my classes in the eleventh grade, even failed summer school. As me and Jonathan got to know each other last summer, I told him how I had decided to turn my life around, but didn't know how I could ever catch up. He offered to help."

"What did he do? Tutor you?" I could imagine him smoothly and easily manipulating Rita, just as he had done to me.

"Not hardly. Since his father is principal, he had access to all the computer security codes. He changed the grades on all my permanent records in the computer, including my SAT scores, so that I could graduate and get into a college. Otherwise, I wouldn't even have had enough credits to get out of the eleventh grade."

"Wouldn't that have got *him* into trouble, instead of you?" I asked.

"Maybe. But he has a way of twisting things so that he looks innocent and you feel stupid and guilty."

"I know." I understood completely.

"But that day I threatened to expose him anyway—about what he had done to me the night before, about everything. He got really angry, snapped out the little silver knife, cut my arm through my track jacket, and told me if I said a word that he would kill me. I believed him."

"So that's when Rhonda and Tyrone found you? I remember them telling me you had a cut on your arm." So much more was clear to me now.

"Yeah. I went home, told my mother as much as she could handle, and we split. Just like that."

"Where'd you disappear to?"

"We've been living with my aunt in Dayton. Her name is Cleopatra Majestic Macmillan. She acts like she's some kind of queen, too. Insists on the very finest, even though she hasn't got a nickel. She's the one who shook me up like I'm trying to do to you, the one who made me see that living and living good is the best revenge."

"So what can I do?" I asked her. "I can't move to Dayton."

"You gotta go back to school—with your head held high. You beat him, Keisha! You won! Let your friends help you. What kind of friend turns her back on folks when they're offering love and support? You may as well smack them in the face just like I did you."

I hung my head. "I didn't want to hurt them. I guess I was just thinking of myself."

"Give them the chance to love you, Keisha. Give yourself the chance to love yourself. And take a shower! You're kinda funky, girl!" Rita laughed, gave me a hug, and marched out of my room as boldly as she had marched in.

"Thanks, Rita," I called to her. "I needed this." As Rita drove away, I opened the window to the early March air that held the slightest hint of spring. I changed the sheets on my bed and cleared the clutter from my room as well as my mind. Edna's words echoed in my mind once again: *Yo' spirit is a shinin' silver star, chile. Can't nobody take that away from you.*

After a shower, with clean hair, clean clothes, and a fresh look on my face, I went downstairs to talk to my mother. "I'm going to school tomorrow," I announced. I know my mother breathed a silent prayer of thanks.

The phone rang, as it had been doing constantly for the last two weeks. Mom sighed and reached over to answer it, but I touched her hand and said, "I'll get it, Mom. I'm ready." Tears filled Mom's eyes. "Hello," I said tentatively.

"Keisha!" It was Rhonda. "Girl, it's *so* good to hear your voice! You feeling better?"

I thought, *It's not like I had the flu or something,* but I just said, "What's going on, Rhonda? You think I flunked the twelfth grade yet?"

Rhonda, glad to be talking about other things, chatted on about the English paper we had to do, the history test, and the leak in the school swimming pool that had flooded the cafeteria. "I'm sure you can catch up. We'll all help you. We got your back, Keisha. You gotta know that."

"I know," I said quietly. "How's the new principal?"

My father had told me that Principal Hathaway had resigned three days after the incident. I knew everybody at school was upset. Mr. Hathaway was really cool—he was fair, and honestly tried to get to know us. I knew that a lot of the students were angry that he had been forced to resign because of the supposed criminal behavior of his son, but I guessed they understood why he had chosen to go.

Rhonda replied, "Girl, you won't believe this. Her name is Emmalina Wiggersly. She's this lemon-faced, pencil-lipped lady, and—get this—she wears this huge wig! And she's mean. Not cool and together like Mr. Hathaway." Then she added, laughing, "She gave Leon detention last week because he wore a wig to school that looked just like hers. It was *too* funny!"

I smiled, knowing how silly Leon would look in a lady's wig, prancing down the hall, mimicking the walk of a woman who was probably tied a little too tightly. "How's Leon?" I asked.

"Going crazy with worry about you," Rhonda told me immediately. "I didn't know how much he cared about you. Do you know he has a whole bulletin board in his room with just your picture on it?"

"Yeah, I found out by accident during Christmas. I really underestimated Leon—all of you, actually. I'm sorry, Rhonda. I just couldn't bear to talk about it—about anything."

"I understand, Keisha. We all do." She paused. "Hey! You feel like shopping? Let's go to the mall!"

Suddenly I was anxious for my world to be normal again, to look for the perfect shoes to match a new outfit, to giggle with my friends about teachers and parents, even to talk about boys. "Oh, yeah! That sounds great. I'm ready to get out of here. Call Jalani—even Angel and Joyelle. Let's get out of here. I need to find something new!"

As soon as I hung up the phone, it rang again. Leon's voice, strong and determined, asked politely, "It's Leon again, Mrs. Montgomery. How is Keisha? Do you think she'll talk to me?"

"Hi, Leon, it's me," I said softly.

Leon was momentarily stunned into silence. "Keisha!" was all he could say. "I've missed you," he said simply.

"I feel like I just got back from a real bad trip, Leon," I told him. "I don't ever want to see the slides or look at the pictures or visit that place ever again."

"Consider it erased," Leon said forcefully.

"I'm going to need some help learning to travel again," I continued, glad to have an easy way to talk about it.

"I'll be your travel agent and your guide if you want me to," Leon offered. "But," he added quickly, "I can just be your friend if that's what you really need."

"I'd like that, Leon," I told him. "Your friendship is real important to me right now." I changed the subject. Emotions made me feel wobbly and unsure. "Hey, Leon! Is it true that you were the one that made the swimming pool leak and flood the cafeteria?"

Leon laughed. "I'll never tell; however, you should know that I prefer dunking my donuts in coffee, not funky pool water!"

I cracked up. It felt cool to laugh again.

"They ought to put you in charge of senior prank this year!"

"My committee has already formulated a plan of attack," Leon responded in a mock falsetto of a business professional. "We shall have an *awesome* senior prank! When are you coming back to school? It won't be any fun unless you're there."

"I'm coming to school tomorrow," I told him, trying to sound confident. "I gotta graduate, and I have lots to do to catch up."

"That's the best news I've had all day!" he told me. "Uh, Keisha?"

"Yeah?"

"Would it be okay if I stopped by in the morning to take you to school? Just in case you needed a little moral support," he added, not trying to push me.

"I'd like that, Leon," I replied. "And Leon?"

"What?"

"I need to apologize to you."

"To me? For what? There is *nothing* that you owe me an apology for!" he said emphatically.

"I'm sorry I lied to you. And I never thanked you for the roses and the necklace. They were so lovely and so special. I thought they were from . . . someone else," I finished uncomfortably.

"You have no need to apologize. Just knowing they made you happy is cool with me."

"The necklace stayed with me through a very dark time, Leon. I never take it off. I just wanted you to know that."

"Thanks, Keisha. I'm glad you told me. And I'm *really* glad you're back! I'll see you in the morning."

I hung up the phone. I was smiling. It had been a long time since I had smiled, and it felt good.

20

April dawned bright and windy. For April Fools' Day, Leon brought a huge bag of seventeen-year locusts to school and released them in the outside courtyard where the underclassmen ate lunch.

"Roaches!" screamed several kids, who knocked over juice bottles and book bags to run from the area. Angel hated bugs of any kind, and she ran screaming with the rest of them.

"Get some bug spray—a gallon of it!" yelled Joyelle. But she was laughing more at the students who were running from the confused insects than trying to get away. "They can't hurt you! They're just disgusting!" Leon peeked his head around the corner and viewed the scene with satisfaction. I was with him, cracking up with laughter. Joyelle saw us, figured we had done it, but said nothing. After all, it *was* April Fools' Day.

"Aren't you scared of bugs?" Leon asked her.

"No. My brother used to chase me with bugs all the time when I was little. I guess I just got used to it," Joyelle explained. "But it was a great prank. Hey, watch your back—here comes the wig lady!"

Leon and I slipped quietly behind the courtyard wall and watched as Ms. Emmalina Wiggersly tiptoed daintily over the mess in the courtyard. Her wig was red today, and slightly askew. She obviously was afraid of bugs, but didn't want the students to see that. "Did you see the perpetrators of this incident?" she asked Joyelle. She always talked like she was a police officer.

"Nope. I didn't see nothing," Joyelle told her.

"Didn't see *anything*," Ms. Wiggersly corrected her.

"You didn't see nothing either?" Joyelle asked with fake innocence. The bell rang then and she giggled and said, "I got to get to class!" She ran from the courtyard in laughter, hurrying to tell Angel what had happened. Ms. Wiggersly remained there alone, checking the bottom of her shoe for insect bodies.

Leon and I ran down the long hall to the senior courtyard, laughing. I felt light and free. It felt good to laugh, be silly, do something stupid. I had been back at school for a month and had caught up with most of the work I had missed while I was out. All of my friends, my teachers, even kids I hardly knew had been helpful and supportive. They let me work at my own speed, and gradually I moved back into senior year. I went to a support group every Saturday, which helped; these were people who had been through the same kind of stuff I had, and because they were strangers, I found it easy to talk to them, to work through some of the rough spots.

The most difficult problem I faced was that Jonathan Hathaway had not been found. He had simply disappeared. His father claimed not to know where he was, and the police had been unable to trace Jonathan at all. There were no credit card receipts to follow, no phone calls to trace, no plane tickets to verify. Jonathan had vanished. This made me unable to completely relax and heal. I was always looking over my shoulder. I was afraid I would see him on the street, at the mall, or in a dark movie theater. Sometimes I would glance up and see a man who was the same height, or had the same build, and I'd gasp in fear. Sometimes I'd hear a voice that was sticky-smooth like honey, and I'd tremble with memories until I was sure that it wasn't Jonathan.

Leon was the rock that he promised he would be. He listened if I needed to talk. He comforted me if I needed to cry. He made me laugh. He asked for nothing for himself, not even attempting to hold my hand unless I offered it first. I needed lots of space, and that's what he gave me.

When we got to the senior courtyard, most of the other seniors were already there. It was the day of the senior meeting, where we got information about prom, caps and gowns, graduation tickets, and other senior concerns. Gerald and Jalani waved for me and Leon to join them. Rhonda sat with Tyrone on the other side. B. J. sat with them.

"Ms. Emmalina Wiggersly might be a bit late," Leon announced, laughing.

"Couldn't find her wig?" Tyrone yelled across the courtyard.

"Ah, now *that's* a good idea for a senior prank!" Leon said devilishly. He seemed to have found his place in the senior class—finally. Instead of being the kid that other kids just laughed at, Leon was the kid who told the best jokes, who pulled the best pranks, who could be depended on to bring the senior class together with laughter. More importantly, Leon was known not really as my boyfriend, which was fine with both of us, but more my special protector—the one who made sure nothing would hurt me or frighten me or upset me. He was real good at that.

Gerald asked, "What *are* we going to do for senior prank, Leon? It's gotta be something better than last year when the seniors dumped sand in the front hall."

"That was stupid," Rhonda said.

"And a mess to clean up," Tyrone added.

Jalani offered, "At the school I went to last year, the seniors made a sculpture out of wet toilet paper and raw eggs. It was supposed to be a hand with two fingers making the sign for victory—a sign the seniors were victorious, I guess. But one of the fingers fell off, and it ended up being an insult and getting them in trouble." She laughed as she remembered the middle-fingered tribute. "Worse than that," she continued, "after two days it really began to stink!"

Leon stood up. "I have an idea that will be remembered for all time—a prank that will be funny, but not messy; memorable, but not destructive—a prank that will make our class stand out as the best one ever!"

"What do you have in mind, Leon?" I asked, giggling a little.

"It's gonna be . . ." At that moment Ms. Wiggersly hurried into the courtyard.

"Seniors! Attention! These are the procedures for an orderly end to the school year. I will insist on decency and decorum and will *not* allow interruptions such as was found in the freshman area today!"

"What did those nasty little freshmen do now?" Leon asked innocently.

She ignored him and continued with her speech. Most of the information she gave us we already knew—dates for the events had been posted since last September. But today she was to announce the results of the senior voting for special responsibilities at graduation. Finally, she cleared her throat and said, "I have the results here of the senior voting. Please give me your full attention."

"You got it!" somebody yelled across the courtyard. She was never quick enough to catch who made the smart remarks, so she just became flustered. The kids enjoyed every minute of it.

Ms. Wiggersly glanced at her paper. "The senior who has been chosen to sing the class song is . . . Leon Hawkins!" Leon looked up with surprise, but bowed with pride and pleasure to the class. By choosing him, they showed him that they had not only noticed him, but accepted him as well. I grinned at him.

"Way to go, Leon!" I whispered as he sat down.

"Almost makes me feel guilty for the prank I've got planned—almost." He grinned at me with a look of mystery.

"What are you going to do?"

"Can't tell you," he whispered back. "That way, if you are captured by the enemy and the wig woman is beating you with her wig, you can't be forced to tell details of our attack plans!"

"You're nuts, Leon." I smacked him on the back of his head.

"I've been trying to tell you that!" he said, crossing his eyes so he looked distorted. "Nobody believes me!"

Ms. Wiggersly continued with her reading of the names. "The invocation and benediction will be given by . . ."

The entire senior class said in unison along with her, "*B. J. Carson!*"

B. J. waved his thanks to the class. "Bless you, my children," he said, grinning.

Ms. Wiggersly cleared her throat. "It seems *that* one was a unanimous decision." She could have smiled then, but she didn't.

She read several more names—the flag bearers, the ushers, the introducers of the school board members who would attend. Ms. Wiggersly said finally, "The last two names are for our student commencement speakers. I am pleased to announce that our valedictorian this year is Nicole Kaywell." She paused as the entire class stood to cheer for Nicole. Being first in the class was something to be celebrated—nobody else had worked that hard, or consistently made the high grades to get to that point. Nicole stood, pleased and blushing with pleasure at the recognition.

"And, as class president, our final speaker will be Miss Keisha Montgomery!"

Once again, everyone stood and applauded, but this time it was for me. I remained sitting, looking amazed. I couldn't understand why they were cheering for me.

"We just want to show you that we all love you, Keisha," Leon told me. "Stand up and wave or something!"

The class was now chanting, "Keisha! Keisha! Keisha!" with loud intensity. Ms. Wiggersly started to try to quiet them down. Then the boys started shouting, *"Seniors! Seniors! Seniors!"* and we all joined them as the bell rang. Ms. Wiggersly gave up. The senior class trooped out of the courtyard, shouting at the top of our lungs, *"Seniors rule! Seniors rule! Seniors rule!"* It was good to be back.

21

The rest of April was a whirlwind for me. The end of the school year seemed to be spinning by. Final school projects, the senior class weekend trip to New York, shopping for a prom dress—all of the activity kept my mind occupied and my thoughts focused on the present and the future. I tried not to linger on the past. I worked on my graduation speech a little each day, alternating between fear about giving it and confidence that I would say just the right thing.

I still went to my support group meetings every Saturday morning, so I liked feeling normal with my closest friends around me in the afternoon. The first Saturday in May was Rhonda's birthday. I'd asked everybody to stop by my house that afternoon to celebrate it. I had bought a small cake at the bakery the day before and stopped to get some chocolate-chunk ice cream, Rhonda's favorite.

I glanced in the mirror as I combed my hair, trying to make it look as if I hadn't been working at it for half an hour to get it just right. I put the brush down for a moment and looked at the girl I saw in the mirror. It had been weeks after the attack before I had been able to look at myself. At first, all I saw in the mirror was shame and fear, pain and dark memories. After a few meetings with my support group, I was able to see just Keisha—a girl with brown skin, brown eyes, brown hair—a girl who could blend into any background. That day, I looked in the mirror and I actually smiled. The face I saw had personality and spunk. My eyes, no longer sunken and depressed, sparkled with anticipation as I looked forward to the afternoon. My hair was not just plain old brown, but a rich auburn, streaked with reddish-brown highlights that showed up in bright sunlight.

I decided to wear a pair of white jeans that I'd bought on a recent shopping trip with Jalani and Rhonda, with a loose-fitting black sweater that I loved. On my neck I wore the silver butterfly necklace. I wore it always; it made me feel safe. I was just putting on a dash of lipstick when the doorbell rang.

Leon was the first to arrive. "What's up, Sunshine?" he said.

"Not much sunshine today—the sky looks like steel wool! I'm glad we didn't decide to do this in the park."

"Springtime weather is so unpredictable," Leon commented, "but I *love* the rain! I like the way it smells when it's over—like grass and dirt."

"There's gotta be something wrong with a dude who likes to smell dirt!" I said wryly.

Gerald and Jalani pulled up into the driveway before I had a chance to close the door. Angel sat in the back seat, holding a wrapped gift. They had stopped by to pick up Monty, who sat next to her. The first drops of rain had started to fall just as they got out of the car. "It's going to rain hard," Gerald noted, checking out the ominously dark sky, "maybe even a thunderstorm."

"This morning I heard the weather reporter say thunder and lightning for sure most of the day," Jalani added.

"Well, I guess I bought her a dumb gift," Monty said with a laugh.

"What did you get her?"

"A kite!"

"As long as she doesn't try to fly it today, she's okay," Angel said as she came into the house. "Now *we* got her something awesome!"

"Whatcha got?" I asked.

"A music box!" Angel said with excitement. "Wait till you see it! It's a little graduate that spins around and plays 'Live Your Dreams.'"

"Wow, what a neat idea—classy," I told her. "Did Gerald pick that out?"

"No way! Me and Jalani picked it out. Gerald wouldn't even go inside the music box store."

"You sayin' I ain't got no class?" Gerald asked.

"I'm just sayin' that you would have picked out a rock and painted 'Happy Birthday' on it!" Angel teased.

"What's wrong with that?" asked Leon, laughing. Gerald nodded in agreement.

The rain and the winds had increased. I switched on the lights in the living room, looking out the window for Rhonda and Tyrone. Monty didn't like thunderstorms, and he stayed very close to me. I saw headlights round the corner, and Tyrone's battered blue Ford rolled down the street and into the driveway. Rhonda and Joyelle ran screaming into the house with newspapers over their heads. Tyrone walked slowly behind them, trying to pretend he didn't care that he was getting wet.

Joyelle was the loudest, as usual. "My hair! My hair!" she squealed as she looked at herself in the hall mirror. The humidity had swollen her hair to twice its size, and the curls she had so carefully done that morning had blown away with the wind. "I give up! I'm just going to shave it bald!"

"Good idea," said Leon, laughing. "Why don't you paint daisies on your head? You could change the design every day to match your outfit!"

"Yeah," Gerald added, "a new fashion trend—all because Joyelle has puffball hair!"

She glared at both of them, then asked me, "Can I run upstairs and use your hair stuff? I gotta fix this!"

"Sure," I replied. "Help yourself." I walked over and gave Rhonda a hug. "Happy birthday, girl. In all this mess, I almost forgot why we're here!"

"Did you remember the chocolate-chunk ice cream?"

"For sure!"

"Then all is forgiven!" We both laughed, then jumped as a rolling clap of thunder filled the room and silenced everyone. The doorbell rang in that moment of silence.

I opened it and there stood B. J., slightly wet and slightly scared. "The thunder rolls and B. J. appears!" I said dramatically.

"What can I say?" B. J. said as he was almost pushed through the doorway by a gust of wind. "I hang with the Thunder Maker."

Just as he said that, the lights in the house flickered and went out. "Watch what you say," I said, half serious and half joking.

"What do we do now?" Monty asked. He was the youngest, and I don't think he wanted to look like a baby in front of the others.

"We'll just sit here and wait till the power comes back on," Tyrone told him. "We can pretend we're on a camp-out."

"Keisha, you got any candles?" Jalani asked.

"Just birthday candles," I said. "My mom told me to get some last week when I went to the grocery store, but I forgot."

Joyelle came down the stairs then, her hair brushed back and tamed for the time being with a couple of rubber bands. "Did I blow a fuse with the hair dryer and the curlers? I didn't have time to finish my hair."

"No, it was the storm. Come and sit down," B. J. said, smiling at her. "You look great."

"I do?"

"Sure."

Joyelle looked at Angel, who gave her that knowing smile that best friends give each other when they know something is going on. B. J. pretended he didn't notice.

The lightning flashed brightly once more, charging the air with light and electricity. The thunder followed almost immediately, rumbling and exploding with huge, frightening blasts.

Tyrone commented, "Thunder makes me nervous, and the only thing that can cure it is chocolate chunk ice cream!"

We all laughed. I said, "Tyrone is right. Let's go ahead and eat. Jalani, help me cut the cake. Then I'll get the ice cream."

"You want me to help?" Angel asked.

"No, you stay there and guard Joyelle's hair in case it escapes!" I laughed as me and Jalani went to the kitchen.

I lit eighteen candles and carried the cake into the living room, where they all waited, sprawled on the floor or the sofa. The soft golden glow of the candles flickered as I moved the cake carefully to the coffee table. I looked at the faces of my friends—Rhonda, happy and hopeful with Tyrone by her side. Jalani, dark, sleek, and sophisticated-looking, comfortably happy with Gerald, whose powerful shoulders offered protection to both Jalani and Angel. Angel, thin and delicate, but healthier now; and Joyelle, who found the joy she needed in the circle of friends around her. B. J., always the loner but never alone, keeping more than just a brotherly eye on Joyelle and her unruly hair; Monty, hungry for attention and friendship, thankful to be included; and Leon, who patiently offered me his strength.

The lightning crackled, the thunder roared, and their voices, small beneath the noise of the wind and storm outside sang:

Happy birthday to you,
Happy birthday to you,
Happy birthday, dear Rhonda,
Happy birthday to you!

Rhonda grinned with pleasure, thanked us all, and blew out the candles in one try. The faint smells of candle wax and smoke floated in the room for a moment, reminding us all of birthdays past, of childhood gone.

"Ice cream!" Monty demanded, breaking the spell. We all laughed and agreed. Monty grinned when he realized that not only was the ice cream chocolate chunk, but the cake was double chocolate chip. "Chocolate can cure anything," Monty mumbled with his mouth full.

"Even thunderstorms?" B. J. asked.

"Makes them easier to take," Monty answered. I think he felt a little better, even though the storm was still loud and forceful outside. We ate our cake and ice cream quietly, listening to the thunder, hoping that the magic of chocolate was real.

I looked at Leon and smiled, a feeling of peace surrounding me in spite of the noise outside.

"Can she open her gifts now?" Monty asked after his third helping of cake. "Mine first!" he insisted. Rhonda, pleased to be the center of attention, sat on the floor with a small pile of gifts in front of her. She glanced at me and smiled. She knew that this party was as much to help me get back to normal as it was to celebrate her birthday. She opened Monty's gift, barely concealed in the thin plastic bag from Kmart.

"Hey, a kite! Awesome! I haven't had one of these since I was kid," she said, giving Monty a hug.

"Can you fly a kite in a tornado?" Monty asked, watching the wind whip the trees outside.

"Probably not a good idea, kid," Tyrone told him, "but it sure would be fun till you got blown away! Here, Rhonda," he said, pushing a small box wrapped in newspaper toward her. "Open this one next."

"Diamonds?" she asked, shaking the box.

"If it was, you just broke 'em, shaking them like that!" Tyrone answered. "Not that you're not worth diamonds, but my budget wouldn't stretch that far."

"Your budget wouldn't know a diamond if it tripped on one!" Gerald teased him.

"What'd you wrap it in newspaper for?" I asked, laughing.

"What is she going to do with the paper? Rip it, right? So why do I have to buy paper for her to tear up? I'd rather spend my money on what's inside!"

As he predicted, Rhonda ripped the paper, and Tyrone gave me a look that said, *See, I told you!* Rhonda carefully opened the box. Inside was a small book entitled, *Smart Quotes by Smart Women for Smart Women*.

"I *love* it!" Rhonda exclaimed, as she flipped through the pages. "This is really cool, Tyrone!"

"Do I get a hug like Monty did?" he asked, grinning. She ran over and gave him a huge bear hug. She started to kiss him, but I think she thought better of it, and ran to sit back down.

Rhonda opened the rest of the gifts, delighted with them all. She loved the little music box from Angel and Gerald, and the blank journal I gave her. The last gift was from Leon. He had forgotten wrapping paper, so he ran upstairs to my bathroom and returned with it wrapped in toilet paper. He gave it to her as if he were presenting a gift from a king. I laughed so hard I almost fell off the sofa.

She opened it and inside were seventy-five packs of bubble gum in dozens of flavors. "Awesome!" Rhonda said, laughing. "This ought to keep me quiet for a year!" She gave everybody a pack of gum to try a flavor.

I said, "You know, graduation is next month, and we might not get another chance to be together like this, all in one place."

"Sure we will—what about the parties?" Jalani offered.

"It's not the same," I insisted. "This is just us. We've been through an awful lot together." Everyone was quiet, agreeing with me, thinking their own thoughts about the past.

Then Leon said, "And for sure we won't get another chance to try to make the biggest bubble gum bubbles in the world!"

"Huh?" Joyelle asked.

"Can you chew a whole pack of bubble gum?" Leon asked excitedly.

"I bet I can," Monty replied with confidence, stuffing four pieces into his mouth.

"The trick is to chew one, get it soft, then chew another and another," suggested Gerald, who was also unwrapping a whole pack of gum.

We all started to giggle and stuff gum into our mouths.

Monty blew a giant cinnamon-red bubble. "Andy used to love bubble gum," he said when it popped. "I'll always remember Andy—the good stuff, not the bad stuff. One day I'll be older than he was when he died. That's weird."

Joyelle could hardly talk because her cheeks were bulging with green apple gum. She laughed and then said quietly, "Life will never be the same without Robbie. But I love my new name and thinking about joy each time I say it. Now I just want to be happy, and

249

have my hair look good three days in a row!" We all laughed.

Angel sat quietly for a moment, the lightning outside making her face flicker from bright to dark. "I think if we don't get rid of the monsters and ghosts and bad stuff, they will eat up our guts. I think I like bubble gum better than gut-sucking ghosts. And I like dancing better than that. One day I'll be a star, and no leftover monster is going to stop me!" Gerald hugged her so fiercely when he heard that he almost made her spit out her gum.

Gerald inhaled, then blew a bright yellow bubble that was bigger than his head. It popped and landed all over his face. Laughing and pulling the pieces off his face, he said, "All I've ever wanted was for Angel to be happy and safe," he said. "I haven't really thought much about me. But I like math, and I'm good with managing stuff, so I'm going to the University of Cincinnati and I'm majoring in bubble gum. If that won't work, I guess I'll major in business. That way, when Angel gets out of college, and she's a star on Broadway, and she's ready to open Angel's School of Ballet, I'll be there to run it for her. Till then, I'll make a lot of money running other people's businesses." Angel beamed and blew a small pink bubble of her own.

Jalani laughed. "My jaws are tired!" She

looked at all of them sitting there in the darkened room. "I feel as if I have known all of you all my life. At a time when I needed friendship—and new shoes—you brought me into your circle and made me one of you." She paused, trying to hold back the tears. "It's impossible to cry and blow a bubble at the same time," she said, half laughing, half crying. "I have found a little sister in Angel, a mother in your mom, Keisha, and yours, too, Rhonda. And I have found someone," she took a deep breath, "whose soul reaches out to mine." Gerald reached out to touch her, but she blew a bubble in his face instead. Laughing, she picked up Monty, and put him on her lap. She started to kiss him on his bubble-gum-puffed cheek.

"Hey, don't be doin' that. I don't like no mushy stuff!" Monty laughed, wiggling out of her lap. "Besides, you got bubble gum on your lips!"

"You're safe, Monty. I was just teasing Gerald," Jalani said as they all laughed at Monty. "He knows how special he is to me." She leaned over and kissed Gerald lightly on the lips.

B. J. announced, but not to anyone's real surprise, "I got my letter of acceptance from Cookman Christian College yesterday. I'm going to be a preacher."

"Well, duh!" Tyrone said. "We all knew

that's what you'd be before you did." B. J. grinned sheepishly.

Tyrone glanced at Rhonda and said, "Well, as long as we're announcing college stuff, I guess I told everybody that I got accepted to Florida A & M—in computer technology. Full scholarship if I play basketball. I can't turn it down. I'm gonna miss all of you, but I don't know how I'm gonna make it without Miss Foxy here."

The thunder continued to rumble, but it seemed to be a little farther away.

Rhonda glanced at him. She knew about his letter, of course, but he didn't know about hers. "Looks like it's show and tell time here for the birthday girl!" She shifted on the pillow she had been sitting on. "I got my letter last week from Howard," she said quietly.

"And you didn't tell me?" Tyrone asked in amazement.

"She told *me*," I teased him.

"Anyway, I was accepted with only a half scholarship. I'm not sure if my folks could handle the rest. We'd have to take on some serious loans."

"So what are you going to do?" Jalani asked. Tyrone looked worried.

"That's not the only place I got accepted." She paused. "I also got accepted to Florida A & M. Full scholarship without sweating like a stinky old basketball player," she teased. "Full academic scholarship! I think I'm gonna major in English—maybe teach poetry to big-headed boys who think they don't like it."

Tyrone looked at her with his mouth open in amazement. A huge wad of purple gum fell out onto the floor. "You did?"

She nodded.

"You're going?"

She nodded again.

Tyrone jumped up and screamed. "Hallelujah! Life is good! Happy birthday, baby!" He picked her up and swung her around, hugging her again and again. All of us cheered at the news.

Leon was quiet. "Even though I got accepted to Morehouse a couple of months ago," he began, "so much has changed since then. I'm not even sure I want to go all the way to Atlanta now. I feel like I'd be leaving behind something that I've looked for all my life." He glanced at me, and I know I was blushing. "I'm majoring in biology—probably with botany as a specialty. At least I'll get easy A's—I already know the name of every single flower in the universe! I'm not sure what I'll do with it yet, but I do know that roses and butterflies will always be my favorites." I fingered the butterfly necklace for the hundredth time that day and smiled at Leon with thankfulness.

"What are you going to do, Keisha?" Jalani asked me.

I smiled at all of them and said, "Just a little while ago, it seemed like I was at the bottom of a pit. I didn't know how to get out." I thought of Edna, and of Rita. I refused to let Jonathan enter my mind. "Now," I continued, "I am out of there and about to be out of here! I think I'm going to go to Miami University—the one here in Ohio, not the one in Florida," I added. "I still plan to be a doctor one day. I want to go away and try it on my own, but I still want to be close to my mom and dad on weekends if I need to come home. I learned the hard way that I don't need to be grown all in one day. I'm gonna take my time." Leon leaned over and kissed me on the cheek. I touched his hand and smiled at him.

The thunder had just about disappeared and the room was starting to feel humid and sweaty when the lights flickered, then stayed on. The CD player upstairs blasted a little too loudly, the air conditioning clicked on, and the dim, dreamy closeness of the last hour somehow disappeared.

"Wow! What a birthday party!" Rhonda exclaimed. "Cake! Ice cream! Thunder! Lightning! Darkness! Bubble gum! You really know how to throw a good one, Keisha."

"Wait till next year," I promised. "I'm working on a tornado for you!"

22

Graduation was one week away. Exams were over, books had been turned in, and final grades had been tallied by the teachers. The school felt empty and very small, as if we no longer fit in the spaces it allowed. The rooms echoed strangely because teachers had taken posters off the walls and returned books to the storeroom. Seniors walked around with yearbooks instead of physics books. Getting signatures became a full-time job as everyone tried to get one from every single member of the class, as well as many of our teachers and friends from other grades. The weather was pleasant, with warm breezes checking out the flowers and trees of late spring.

The last day for seniors was traditionally

the day of the senior breakfast—as well as the senior prank. All of us came dressed in our sharpest threads—new hookups for the summer with plans and hopes for the fall. Many of the seniors had chosen to go to college, many of them right at home at the University of Cincinnati, or Cincinnati State. Others chose schools all over the country. A few kids went into the military, and some decided to go right to work, but all of us were excited at the prospect of getting out.

After the breakfast of rubbery eggs and crunchy sweet rolls in the cafeteria, we all trooped to the overheated auditorium for recognition and awards. Scholarships were announced. Certificates were given for various accomplishments. A boy named Bruce Bingington had had perfect attendance from kindergarten through twelfth grade. The senior class gave him a special presentation—a certificate that said, "To the student who *ought* to be the smartest, since he never missed a day!" He accepted it and told us, "I started to skip school today, since it was the last chance I would ever have, but I'm glad I showed up!" We all laughed.

After the awards, the seniors were traditionally allowed to go home early. But instead of dismissing us, Ms. Emmalina Wiggersly stepped to the podium. Her wig, as usual, was just a little crooked. "I have a few words I would like to say to this class," she began in her high nasal voice. "Although I have only known many of you for a short time, I am appalled at the extreme *lack of maturity* that I found among members of this class! I expected more from a group of seniors." She looked down at her notes. "First of all, those perpetrators who removed the 'For Sale' signs from homes in the neighborhood and put them on the lawn of the school must remove them at once and return them to their rightful places! I am *not* amused!"

"I am!" a voice from the crowd cried out.

"Secondly," she continued, talking much too close to the microphone, "I am appalled by your incredible lack of respect to the junior class!"

"They ain't s'posed to get no respect! They're juniors!" The entire class laughed in agreement. The rivalry between the junior and senior classes had been going on for years. As a newcomer, Ms. Wiggersly couldn't understand that.

"Finally," she intoned into the microphone, "your misuse of school property is almost criminal!" She paused and cleared her throat. "I am referring to the case of school toilet paper that was used to line the halls yesterday. The perpetrators will be punished!"

"Probably by making them use that

stuff," Leon whispered to me, laughing. "School toilet paper should be classified as a deadly weapon—that stuff can slice through steel!"

"Why can't she compliment us on the good stuff we do?" Rhonda complained. "Like our volunteer projects or our date-rape counseling center?"

Leon looked around at the seniors, who all looked to him for the signal. "We're gonna have to do it," he said. "She just can't come in here and dis us like this!" He nodded his head and said quietly, "Let 'em roll!"

Thousands of marbles spilled from pockets, purses, and plastic bags that had been hidden under the seats in the auditorium. The noise was deafening, along with the roaring of the laughter of the seniors, the tiny glass balls rolling swiftly down the aisles directly to the spot where Ms. Emmalina Wiggersly stood. She screamed and ran up the steps to the stage.

"I will find the perpetrators of this crime!" she squeaked. The bell rang, and the seniors gave a mighty cheer and marched out of the auditorium.

"That was *awesome*, Leon," everyone told him as they hurried out of the school. "And the 'For Sale' signs and toilet paper, too." He grinned with pride.

I ran up to him and hugged him. "I'll help

you get the signs back tonight," I reminded him. "Did you get enough money for the collection for the custodians?"

"Yeah, everybody was cool. We got plenty to give them something extra for sweeping up the marbles and the paper. I'd do it myself, but I might be labeled a 'perpetrator'!" He laughed again. "See you tonight!" He ran to get his car.

"You going home now?" I asked Rhonda.

"No, girl, let's go shopping," Rhonda suggested.

"You want to come, Jalani? Let's go to the mall to get dresses to wear under our robes at graduation."

"I'm in!" Jalani said cheerfully. "Let's blow this place!" She laughed. "It's full of 'perpetrators'!" We drove to the mall with all the windows down and the music up. We sang as loud as we could and rolled with freedom to the mall.

"I remember seniors from past years complaining about how hot those graduation robes can be," I said as we strolled through the aisles of the first store. "What about this dress?" I asked them.

"That looks like something your mama would wear!" Rhonda laughed and I dropped it instantly. "This is cute, though." Rhonda added, feeling the fabric of a slim red dress.

"I think red dresses make you look fat,"

Jalani teased. Rhonda put the dress back on the rack.

We each picked out several dresses, went to the dressing rooms to try them on, then, still undecided, went to another store to see if they had a better selection.

"Look at this!" Jalani said in amazement. "This same dress was twenty dollars more in that other store!"

"They're always jacking up the prices like that," I complained.

"That's why I like making my own clothes," Jalani said. "But sometimes I just want something quick and easy that someone else made." She sighed and picked out two more dresses.

I found a dress—all white—that I liked right away. "I think I'll try this one," I said before either of the other girls could grab it.

"That's sharp," Rhonda commented.

I tried it on and it was perfect—pale and shimmery, light and thin. It seemed to float on me rather than weigh me down. "It makes me feel like a butterfly," I told Rhonda and Jalani as I modeled it for them.

They agreed, and I bought it, feeling very satisfied with myself. Rhonda did the best of all of us—she found a slim black sleeveless dress to wear under her gown and a sharp little skirt and top of pale turquoise to wear sometime during the summer to impress

Tyrone. But Jalani couldn't find anything that satisfied her. She decided to wait, or go ahead and make something based on the styles she saw today. She had magic fingers—she could make a dress in one night.

"I'm hungry!" I said finally. "Let's all go to my house. My mom made some lasagna to die for!"

"I'm with you, girl," Rhonda agreed. "Shopping takes it out of me!"

"Shopping ought to be an Olympic sport!" Jalani added, laughing. "It takes a well-fed athlete to do it right! So let's do the lasagna thing."

We chattered and giggled as we drove to my house. Surprisingly, both my parents were at home—Daddy had taken a couple of vacation days, and Mom had decided to take a day off with him. It was kinda nice to have them home in the middle of the day. Jalani made lemonade, Rhonda made a salad, and I heated up the lasagna. There was more than enough for all of us. Daddy teased Jalani and Rhonda about our shopping trip and asked them about college plans and such. Mom seemed to be glad to have a house full of giggling girls— making the normal noisy sounds that girls are supposed to make.

The doorbell rang and Mom ran to get it. "Are you expecting anyone else, Keisha?" she asked me.

"I don't think so," I said.

Mom called with an edge of alarm in her voice, "Victor, I think you better come here." Daddy wiped his mouth and ran to the door. Rhonda, Jalani, and I followed.

I gasped and stared. Standing at our door, looking somehow much older and more worn about his face, was our former principal Mr. Hathaway. It seemed as if time stood still. The smell of the lasagna, the laughter of just a few minutes ago—all of that disappeared as I tried to calm myself. I felt dizzy—like I might throw up.

No one had seen Mr. Hathaway since he had resigned. He and his wife had moved from their home, even though it had not been sold. They had an unlisted phone number and stayed away from all of the places they used to go. And still no one had seen Jonathan.

My mother took a deep breath and said finally, "Hello, Mr. Hathaway." She didn't smile.

"May I come in, please?" He looked as if he was about to cry.

My father frowned, but he said, "Come in. Have a seat."

We all sat in the living room—waiting. Finally, Mr. Hathaway sighed and looked directly at me. He said, "First of all, although I know it means very little, I am so very sorry— for everything. Keisha, there is no way I can say enough to apologize to you."

"I'm learning to get on with my life, Mr. Hathaway," I said quietly.

"There are some things that you should know," he continued. "I have been meaning to come to your house, but I've been so overwhelmed with recent problems that I just couldn't. Again, let me apologize."

"What do you want to tell us?" my father asked. Rhonda and Jalani had scooted their chairs closer so they could hear what he was saying.

Mr. Hathaway began as he cleared his throat, "Jonathan *did* come to our home that night . . . the night of the Valentine's Dance," he began. "His face was badly cut, and he was almost hysterical. He refused to go to a hospital. I forced him to tell me what had happened." He sighed.

"Did he tell you everything?" I asked harshly. "Did he tell you that he tried to rape me? Did he tell you that I cut his face trying to get away from him? *Did he?*" I was almost yelling, hating that I had to remember once again.

Mr. Hathaway bowed his head. "Yes, he told us everything, dear. I'm just so very sorry . . ."

"Quit apologizing!" I yelled. Then I said, more quietly, "It's not really your fault."

"This was not the first time he had done this," he said sadly.

"I know," I said coldly. "Why didn't you get him some help—do something to stop him?" I demanded.

"I tried. The last therapists we had him with said that his inclinations were under control. That was six years ago."

"Tell that to Rita Bronson!" I said harshly.

"Rita Bronson? Another attack? I didn't know about her." Mr. Hathaway sighed with great sorrow.

"Where is he now?" my father demanded. "He needs to be in jail!"

"That's where he is," Mr. Hathaway said sadly. "Let me explain. That night, his stepmother, who is a doctor, was able to put the necessary stitches in his face. I drove him to Lexington, Kentucky, where I have cousins. I know it was wrong, but he is my son," he added simply.

"So how did he end up in jail?" I asked.

Mr. Hathaway continued. "Jonathan was devastated about his face. He is very vain, and he worried about having a scar." I smiled with grim satisfaction. "His face had barely healed," Mr. Hathaway continued slowly, "before he was out every day, hanging around the local high school, trying to charm the young ladies."

"Why didn't you have him locked up?" my mother demanded.

"You can't get arrested for talking to girls,"

Mr. Hathaway explained gently. "According to my cousin, who found out about all this later, Jonathan tried to use his usual smooth style with the high school girls there, but most of them ignored him—maybe because of the cut on his face. A fifteen year old named Candy, however, must have fallen under his spell in spite of the scar." Mr. Hathaway breathed deeply and looked at the floor.

"He took her to a motel room . . ."

I bet it smelled like lavender, I thought.

". . . and he assaulted her." The silence in my living room was thick as mud.

"Did he use a knife?" I asked.

"Yes, the silver knife his mother gave him when he was eight years old," Mr. Hathaway said sadly. "He loved that knife—carried it with him always. It was the only gift she ever gave him."

"Jonathan is very sick, Mr. Hathaway," my father said.

"I know. He will be in prison for quite a while. His sentence for the attack on the girl in Kentucky was thirty years, with no chance of parole before that."

Inwardly, I sighed with relief. It was as if a dark storm cloud had been lifted from me, as if I hadn't breathed since that horrible night in February. "Thank you for telling us this, Mr. Hathaway. I'm glad I don't have to live the rest of my life looking over my shoulder to see if Jonathan is behind me."

He stood to leave then. He shook my parents' hands and gave me one last, thoughtful look. "Good-bye, Mr. Hathaway," I said. "I'll be fine." I remembered Edna's words once more: *Yo' spirit is a shinin' silver star, chile. Can't nobody take that away from you.*

Outside, the sun was bright, the air was soft and pleasant, and no clouds could be seen in the pale blue sky.

FINALE

We waited in the darkness for the signal to begin. I wondered what was taking so long. I heard someone whispering behind me. Our silky gowns were rustling softly as we, the graduating seniors, adjusted our hats, hair, and nerves. We stood nervously in two lines that curved from the back of the auditorium out into the hallway halfway up a flight of stairs. We were in alphabetical order for the very last time, the boys in gowns of navy blue, the girls in silver.

I was one of the first in line because I had to sit on the stage. Even though it was hot, I was shivering in the darkness while we waited for the lights to come up to announce the beginning of the ceremony. I closed my eyes, but the darkness seemed like it was trying to grab me. I blinked, and the shadows were breathing on my neck, chasing through my thoughts.

I let the shadows walk me back through the last two years, through loss, pain, death, and humiliation. Dark memories of fire and blood were running in slow motion through my head. I thought about Rob, who died in that car crash in November of our junior year. I thought about my Andy, my dear sweet Andy, who left me—left us all—the following April. And I tried not to think about my own dark stain.

Like silent trumpets, the lights of the auditorium suddenly blazed. We seniors cheered, the audience stood and applauded, and then we heard the tinny sound of "Pomp and Circumstance" coming from the school orchestra sitting at the front. I always cry when I hear that song. As we marched proudly down the aisle, our excited parents flashing cameras and waving with joy, I thought back to my first day of school as a kindergartner, how scared I was and how a skinny little boy named Andy Jackson shared his peanut butter sandwich with me. I thought about grade school and long division, junior high and locker partners, high school and basketball games, hospitals and funerals.

As senior class president, I had to give a

speech, but I didn't know if I could stand in front of that huge room of parents and students and put the shadows into words. I climbed the steps slowly—this was no time to trip or stumble—and I watched the others march in. The rest of the graduates proudly filed into rows of gowns and hats into the seats in front of me, their faces were unwrapped packages of smiles and success. We sat down, the lights were dimmed, and the ceremony began with the usual speeches from school board members and declarations by the principal. My speech was the very last of the evening—our final good-bye. I held the pages tightly in my hand as I skimmed the words once more. I tried to relax a little, and I grabbed the tiny butterfly hanging from the thin silver chain around my neck. When it was time, I was ready.

"And now, ladies and gentlemen, please welcome our final speaker of the evening: our senior class president, Miss Keisha Montgomery, who will deliver the parting address from the senior class," I heard Ms. Wiggersly say. Every member of the senior class stood and applauded as I walked slowly to the podium. I felt their strength and I didn't cry. I knew my parents, sitting out there in the audience with Monty, Angel, and Joyelle, were probably shedding a couple of tears. I breathed slowly and evenly as I adjusted my eyes to the brightness of the stage lights and the darkness of the auditorium in front of me. I was not afraid.

I began: "We, the members of this graduating class, are joined together forever in a circle of friendship and memories. We have read of death in our history books; we have seen death's face up close. We have studied the problems of society; we have seen how those problems can devastate a friend. Because of our unusual difficulties, we have become stronger. Our shared tears have become the glue that binds us together in love.

"Two members of our graduating class will not be marching out of this room with us tonight. They will not go to college, or marry, or discover a cure for cancer. Andy Jackson and Robbie Washington are forever silent, but never forgotten. Their spirit lives with each of us, in each of us, and joins us together in this powerful circle of love.

"Let us not leave this place in sorrow, however. Our spirits are too strong to dwell only in the past. Let us take our spirits now, like the flames of many candles, to a new world, a world of hope and possibilities, a place where butterflies are magic and dreams can never die.

"I would like to ask the senior class to stand now, and to join hands—all of you." The seniors looked around in slight confusion, but obeyed, joining hot and sweaty hands together for what was surely their very last time together. They looked up at me with expectation.

"I wrote this poem when I came back to school this spring." My voice stammered a bit. "It is called, 'Let Our Circle Be Unbroken.'" I paused, breathed deeply, and began. "Please repeat after me," I said. "Let our circle be unbroken."

"*Let our circle be unbroken,*" they repeated, their voices loud and strong.

let our joys and sorrow sing
let our joys and sorrow sing
let all children hear our message
let all children hear our message
let our mighty spirits bring
let our mighty spirits bring
all the power of the seniors
all the power of the seniors
all our dignity and pride
all our dignity and pride
let our circle be unbroken
let our circle be unbroken
as we clasp our hands and guide
as we clasp our hands and guide
all our voices to the heavens
all our voices to the heavens
as each hand to hand is pressed
as each hand to hand is pressed

and our love and will is strengthened
and our love and will is strengthened
and our minds and bodies blessed
and our minds and bodies blessed
by the power of the ancients
by the power of the ancients
and the wisdom of the winds
and the wisdom of the winds
let our circle be unbroken
let our circle be unbroken
for our circle never ends
for our circle never ends

The seniors cheered, holding their hands together high above their heads. The lights brightened the room again, the orchestra began to play, and the trumpets sounded. And all of us, the senior class, clutched our diplomas, left the shadows of the past behind us, and marched proudly out of the auditorium into the dawn of our tomorrows.

A READERS' GUIDE TO *DARKNESS BEFORE DAWN*

Darkness Before Dawn is the third book in a trilogy that includes *Tears of a Tiger* and *Forged by Fire*. Sharon M. Draper says that the reason she wrote the third book was the hundreds of letters she had received from young readers who had embraced the characters in *Tears of a Tiger* and *Forged by Fire*. "What happened to Keisha?" they asked. "Did she ever find happiness? And what about Gerald and Angel? How did they cope after the fire? Did Rhonda and Tyrone stay together or break up?"

Darkness Before Dawn answers all of these questions and more. Keisha, Rhonda, Tyrone, Gerald, and B. J. are all in their senior year. Gerald's little sister Angel and Rob's younger sister Joyelle are both ninth graders, excited to be in the first year of high school. Rhonda and Tyrone are still together and trying to deal with the closeness of their relationship. Keisha, lonely and still trying to cope with the loss of Andy, envies what they have.

Several new characters add mystery, excitement, and humor to the school year. Jalani, a transfer student, is tall, lovely, and drives her own bright red BMW. Gerald admires her from afar. Leon, the class clown, hides a secret, and Jonathan Hathaway, the principal's son and the new student teacher, becomes much more than the track coach.

Darkness Before Dawn promises to be a strong and satisfying conclusion to the story of a group of characters that have become too real to forget.

Discussion Topics
• *Darkness Before Dawn* begins at the end (Keisha's high school graduation) and then takes the reader back to April of the characters' junior year in high school. It is told in first person, from Keisha's point of view. What is the advantage of having a story told in first person? What is the disadvantage?

• A *motif* is a word or image that is repeated throughout a novel that helps to highlight or unify a central idea. Trace the references to the use of the word "silver" in the novel and explain how silver is important to the development of the story.

• Even though Keisha is intelligent and mature, she is easily entangled in Jonathan Hathaway's trap. Explain how this occurs and discuss whether you think Keisha's mistakes are realistic.

• Discuss the role of Edna. Why is she significant, even though she is a very minor character? What does she teach Keisha and Jalani about people who are homeless and/or needy? What is meant by her statement, "Yo spirit is a shinin' silver star, chile. Can't nobody take that away from you"?

• Discuss the character of Jonathan Hathaway. Does he have any redeeming qualities, or is he purely a negative character? What might have made Jonathan the person he became?

• Discuss the character of Leon. What makes him a positive character? Why is he good for Keisha, and why does she initially reject him? How did his background affect his personality?

• Discuss Joyelle and what you thought about her name change. What was the effect of her name change on how she dealt with the problems she faced? Did changing her name really make a difference? Explain how she managed to crash her father's car and why you think she did it.

• Discuss the characters of Rhonda and Tyrone. Discuss how they manage to control their emotions, as well as their reactions to those feelings, in spite of the intensity of the feelings they have for each other.

• In chapter fourteen of *Darkness Before Dawn*, the kids are at Rhonda's house doing homework on poetry.

Summarize their discussion, then write a poem about some aspect of one of the three books of the Hazelwood High trilogy. Analyze the poem at the very end of the book. How is it effective for the message Keisha wants to give?

• Keisha is searching for "a real man—someone who is mature and sophisticated" throughout the story. What qualities are found in "a real man"? Discuss each of the male characters in the story (include students as well as adults) and tell how they fit your qualifications.

• Keisha says at the end of *Darkness Before Dawn*, "We, the members of this graduating class, are joined together forever in a circle or friendship and memories. Because of our unusual difficulties, we have become stronger. Our shared tears have become the glue that has bound us together in love." Explain what she means. How are difficulties in life sometimes useful for making people grow closer together?

• Explain the title of the novel. What was the "darkness" in the lives of not just Keisha, but all of the characters? Why did it have to come before the "dawn" in their lives? How would you describe the "dawn"? Explain how the title might apply to a real-life situation.

Suggested Activities
• You are a reporter at one of the following scenes. Write a story for your newspaper.
-The first day of school in any American high school
-Graduation day in any large American high school
• In diary form, write the life of Edna for several months. Include details about how she managed to live her life.
• Friendship is extremely important in *Darkness Before Dawn*. Discuss the friendships of the following people:
-Keisha and Rhonda

-Joyelle and Angel
-Leon and Keisha
-Jalani and Gerald
-Monty and Keisha
-Jalani and Rhonda

• Write a magazine article about Jalani. Include her life in Africa, her relationship with her parents and her new stepmother, the death of her mother, and her relationship with her new friends. Include drawings of Jalani's clothing designs if you like.

• Write a biography of Jonathan Hathaway, focusing on his childhood. Include details about his mother, his father, and his thoughts while growing up.